D1201478

Low Tide

Low Tide

FERNANDA EBERSTADT

Alfred A. Knopf   New York   1985

THIS IS A BORZOI BOOK
PUBLISHED BY ALFRED A. KNOPF, INC.

Library of Congress Cataloguing in Publication Data

Eberstadt, Fernanda,   Low tide.

I. Title.
PS3555.B484L6 1985   813'.54   84-48655
ISBN 0-394-54429-3

Manufactured in the United States of America

FIRST EDITION

Low Tide

One

My father left my mother when I was twelve and went back to London. I had always pictured that Mummy in turn would go home to Louisiana on this longed-for End of Days, for she had raised me on stories of the Great House at Terrebonne: a tottering Third Empire delirium of glory-be, giddy with pinnacles and cupolas, a house of cards which wailed in a high wind, swayed like a lily in a hurricane, and sweated and blistered under a noonday heat that was like the Hand of God coming palm down on you. And beyond its tiny preserve, mangrove swamp throbbing with mosquitoes and a river thick as mud whose motionless murk curvetted all the way to the Isles Dernieres. Mummy had fed me on these stories of the house and its doings, which were stories of the heart's blood, as a pelican feeds its young, or so the legends say. She had raised me chanting the rivers of the South: the Calcasien and the Pascagoula, the Amite and the Boeuf, the Sabine that divides Louisiana from Texas, and the Mississippi which shoulders past New Orleans with such purpose only to expire into gray sand and trickling deltaway at Pilottown. But there was no such black bayou any more, no such house, only what she had invented to keep muggers out of her mind.

So we stayed on in New York after Daddy left, Mummy, Eustacius, and me, in a brownstone house on East 94th Street, where nothing of mine was swept away. In the kitchen, the walls were decked with Halloween masks, steamed labels from Haitian cocoa powder, hot-colored fetishes. In the garden there were still the rotten spars of the tree house like a crazed aircraft pitched among the weeds.

When the tide goes way out, sometimes odd sea things are stranded in the sand. Sea calves, sea horses, too-many-legged crabs. In the Renaissance, men thought everything on land had its sea partner: sometimes we get drowned and they get beached. Jem and I, Mummy, Mrs. Palafox, Eustacius, are such creatures—landed, salt-dried, and petrified in our monstrousness.

Eustacius was an old black man.

"*How* old, Eustacius?"

"Well, I don't know *exactly*, but old enough to know better."

He knew better than anyone. He had blacked boots in my great-grandmother's house when he was a little boy until he had been apprenticed to the cook, who was so fat that she died. He had had three wives, one mad like my Aunt Celestine. He was a magical dancer; he could do the samba and just to see him wiggle a hip was a marvel. He was a lucky gambler; he knew where the silver ball would stop its whirl. He knew the aces in any pack, no matter how often you shuffled, but he was a righteous Baptist. He couldn't read, but second sight told him things books do not divulge. Strange angels told him things in visions that they told no one else. One of these angels was my Aunt Celestine, who came to him at night chattering like a macaw (although she died in a home in New Orleans when she was nineteen). "Oh, that Miss Celestine," said Eustacius some mornings. "She something else again. She kept me up last night, laughing over them old stories and carrying on till *dawn*. I dead tired today, but we had a *fine* time for sure."

Aunt Celestine told him whom the Lord would take and who would be spared. He could see the devils clamoring like parrots from men's shoulders and hiding behind doors, and he could tell who was good at a glance. He didn't like men hanging around my mother's house after Daddy was gone; he thought she should go and bring him back. "You daddy's a gentleman. You mother should thank her lucky stars to have found a good man like Mr. Western."

My grandmother hadn't thought so when Mummy first brought this pink-and-gold flit back to the house, an Englishman she had picked up at Cousin Mimi's coming-out party— well, Big Mimi was always very fast. She put her hands over her ears when my father delivered his piercing giggle, and said to my mother, "Pomelia, it's beyond me how a fellow can be both a gigolo and a fairy."

But it was a manner like any other, this flutiness, and the festive unconcern with which he ran their marriage. They lived as if the bailiff were coming in the morning; they gave extravagant parties every night, and Daddy didn't seem to care whether thirty people showed up for a dinner of Baby Ruths and blue movies, or didn't show up at all because they had decided instead to hire a white Cadillac and drive to Rockaway Beach. It wasn't until long after Daddy left and the house had fallen into irreversible disrepair that I realized how carefully life had been arranged and understood that forced gaiety after all couldn't save the day.

Mummy had been the disruptive fluke in my father's composition. She swung from impulse to impulse; she didn't know what she did. There were times when she was likely to empty her pocketbook out the window to see the twenties fly away, to give her evening dresses to transvestites; she was likely to barricade herself in her room during dinner parties, smoking in the dark. If coaxed to come to parents/teachers meetings, she would trail instead into the middle of my art class in blue jeans and a sable coat, her hair coiled up in an enormous nest of braids and red anemones. And she would squeeze me and hang on to my arm while I was supposed to paint, and plead extravagantly, almost tearfully, with my art teacher to be allowed to take the picture home. "No, Mrs. Western, I'm afraid all the work must stay here for the Parents' Day exhibit." But Mummy would steal my picture anyway and paste it on the kitchen wall, every morning a blazing reminder of shame.

She was tall, tall, tall, my mother, and gaunt as John the Baptist, with a brown face all hollow cheeks and violet circles scored under hollow eyes. But she had a sweet smile, showing pearly little teeth, so sweet it made you see stars. Her closet was the size of a lion's den. You could walk down the aisles, looking at each sequined miniskirt, each white leather safari suit. And a museum of shoes. But she always wore the same baggy blue jeans that didn't quite hit the ankles of her long legs, and the same old holey black sweater. She made lairs about the house with trails leading to them; a spoor of black sweaters dropped along the way as she traveled lighter, of frozen daiquiris in which the ice had trickled bluish causeways through the banana and rum sludge.

And my father got more fractious. He snapped when she was gay and teasing and he liked it no better when she lay in a darkened room all day, in a rat's nest of black cashmere. The sight of her straying down the sidewalk in dark glasses, bumping into trees, was enough to make him boil.

"Oh lordy," sighed my mother, sardonically.

And so he went back to London at last and became an art dealer.

And Eustacius came out of the kitchen and took over. He was a real man.

His dinners were not like dinners at other people's houses,

where ladies drink white wine on ice, anesthetized (Eustacius served bourbon and rum, and told me of times when he had made three hundred mint juleps for a dinner party), where food is glassed in like museum exhibits, served up on an operating table to be picked at with steel chopsticks. Why do they imprison them so, the little animals mounted in jellies and crushed in ices, the vegetables and fruits mangled to a nursery sauce, as if, merely boiled or grilled, the dead things could escape. When Eustacius served crayfish, you could still see their expressions.

When Eustacius cooked, it was voodoo each time. It was no good Mummy's sitting down with him to say, "Mr. and Mrs. Diaz and the Cravens and Mr. Fox are coming over on Wednesday, so we would like dinner at nine. That black bean soup to start, then the soft-shell crabs, and floating island for dessert."

You never knew what would turn up or how. He threw in a mess of things, different each time, and mucked it around. A load of spices, a shot of booze: a gumbo melée. If it appeared by nine, it was by accident. If it was black bean soup, it was because inspiration had not turned up.

And then dinner was served up as before disdainful gods, on a lacquered altar flaming with candles. His idea of amenities was macabre: paper rosettes on squabs' legs, gardenias in the fingerbowls.

He liked flambées and soufflés: things doused in spirits that rise and flame in the night. He liked things he could only get in the Cajun market in Queens: charred crayfish, okra, tiny snails to stick in omelettes, and soft-shell crabs you could crunch whole.

"Heady," said Eustacius. "That soup real heady." And it was his grandest praise. But beware lest my dress be too heady, for he would tell me, "Men going to look backwards at you in that piece of nothing."

"It's not nothing. It's mousseline."

"It something, all right—it sinful. It sinful to wear you shift outdoors when you a big girl."

People came to dinner with envelopes for Eustacius—notes he couldn't read; but there was much to be gleaned from a letter without knowing its alphabet. He pinned down its author by the swoops and curves and judged the contents by underlinings and dashes.

"I read *between* the lines," he told me. And you didn't need to know how to read to welcome long-parted friends: Jefferson who was high compliments, Grant most gracious thanks.

Eustacius liked the ladies like willow trees, the stern men. He could smell old money.

Mummy's drugged film makers, Daddy's snappy South Americans, Eustacius called parrots and gaudies.

"It don't show you great-grandmother plates respect to let they flimsies eat off them."

He adored it when the men got sozzled on his mint juleps, but as soon as he thought Mummy had had enough he would trot out to the living room and call her aside.

"You do respect to you body, Mrs. Pomelia, even if you let you soul go fly away. Don't let me see you droop like a Raggedy Ann doll. It make me *tired*."

"Eustacius is an old mule," complained Mummy. "He revels it up on bourbon on the sly until he's so soused he can scarcely serve. So why can't *I* ever go to town?"

There was this I had no use for in Eustacius, or in Daddy either: they talked propriety and good appearances, they extolled the silver-voiced ladies, but they married mad girls. They didn't restrain their wild things, either, but stung them madder. And let them go their ways not for stately living, no, but for still more abandoned creatures.

And thus it was my great-grandmother that Eustacius always invoked, but wayward Celestine he loved too much to speak of, except as she came to him in visions. I know he and Mummy would talk and cry about her sometimes, but he wouldn't talk to me about the past.

"You too smart to trouble with people on the other side of the divide."

The divide, the great divide. It gaped between night and waking deed, quick and dead. It was an edict confining me to the sane and self-ruled, while Mummy and Celestine and maybe Eustacius even, were left smiling and waving from a far delicious orient shore.

One thing Eustacius looked forward to, and that was my coming-out party. He told me stories about it when I was little, about that magnificent night when I would be presented to society.

"And then you have lace all down to you toes, lace to you little satin feet, and all magnolias in you yellow hair. And they all see you there, such a shining spectacle, and they stare and stare—the families with they handsome boys in black—and the waltzes run on until it pink outside and everybody laugh and laugh, and the champagne bubbles run out the door. . . ."

How could I be awed by Judgment Day when such a night was closer at hand? My birthday parties were greedy anticipations of that night, for I didn't like girls, but invited instead fifty boys—not in black, it is true, but blue velvet and lace collars. Ice cream in molds like lions, tigers, elephants. Continents of cake. But no waltzes, and nannies took their charges home long before it grew pink outside or even black. I remember my delight at the boy who cried when the lights went out. You can never tell what will amuse children, and even less what will embarrass or frighten them. I went to sleep in disgust at the circus but screamed in terror at the ballet, at the dancers whose bound feet were not silent but thudded across the stage as if trampling dead birds under.

I remember best being bored when I was little, more often and worse than I will ever be again. I remember being itchy all over and wriggling in red velvet seats and finally crawling under the table to go to sleep.

I remember when I stopped being bored, too. There comes a moment at which we are made aware of the separate lives of other people, sometimes in a grand gesture of the imagination, sometimes from the inexorable pressure of the outside forcing itself in. It can be terrible. For me, it was a joyful recognition that other human beings were not as pasteboard and spangled as I had thought, that they cried without knowing why, and remembered their dreams the next morning. And that beyond that mass of sloppy feelings there was a marked tribe, secret, which went the chosen way, unrelenting. You recognized them on the street without a flicker. The Chasms were the first I met. Mrs. Chasm was half dead or abroad and the boys still lay in store, so it was Professor Chasm who came alive to me, and I could discard the rest of the universe. Professor Chasm was my father's oldest friend.

"Charlie was a school hero," Daddy told me. "A skirt chaser and an able scholar. Charlie could drink like an Eskimo, bang anything that would stand still long enough (and talked up a storm about it afterwards), and on the necessary occasions he would stagger into the examination halls and walk out again with all the prizes. As for me, I was just a goose: an English Catholic—a strange breed, lovey—with weak ankles, weak stomach, and a stutter, who adored his three sisters and his nanny, and never thought to harbor an indecent intention toward a girl."

But I think this legend had its slant, for, while Chasm stayed on at Oxford doing graduate work, it was Daddy who had come to America when he was twenty-one. Scavenger days from a rented room in lower Manhattan peddling snuff-boxes in his grand accent and his one good suit. The long-delayed score was Miss Pomelia, but Daddy by then was a confirmed bachelor and self-willed, not at all the malleable innocent he imagined. He thrived on company, and possessive clutching gave him the vapors. She never wanted to go out. And she was jealous. A termagant. Incurable. And so my father began again in London after what proved a most amiable parting, despite my grandmother's assessment of his character and profession, not having made even a nick in Mummy's fortune. "What fortune?" he demanded irritably. "Those conceited southern profligates haven't got poker chips for money. As a matter of fact, I've most likely spared you the alms house with what economies I've managed to smuggle past your mother's voracious eye."

What had Charlie Chasm ever done with himself? He had gone on to teach at Oxford, prising fellowships and university posts from tight fists, and come to America when he was thirty. He was made a professor of politics at the age of thirty-five and had since come into a minor renown: he lectured and toured and went to conferences and turned out a book every year. He wrote books that people could savage without having read and articles they could read on planes. He wrote about the terrorist import-export business and Soviet activities in Latin America. He had a grand Mexican wife who never went out, and he came to my parents' parties alone (which was fine with Eustacius, who had had it to the eyeballs with keeping dinner waiting for bedizened spics who sauntered in at midnight). He had a taste for fast society, but he never fitted in: that was why he was mine. The money that accompanied Professor Chasm's wife and his career seemed a freak that never removed the holes in his socks or the tape holding his spectacles together. It was the tatters and the tape that were real. When he came to our house when I was little, I never believed that he had left a wife and two children behind. Were they waiting up for him? Such trappings could only debase his raffish, foulmouthed manliness. I willed him to like me better than them.

He was a lame mongrel who in spite of his long, jutting bones held me just the right way, smelled of tobacco to his fingertips and not eau-de-cologne like my father, and had blue stubble on his cleft chin that scratched agreeably. I hid under the table as the grown-ups came in to dinner, and I knew that he would crawl under the table to talk to me and that Daddy wouldn't send me back to bed. "What do you make of all this foolery going on above our heads, sailor boy?"

"I like the green noodles and that's all."

"Shall I nab you a plate when they come along?"

"Everyone would think you were a sea monster. You look like Heathcliff. You have a hole in your chin like Heathcliff did."

"How do you know he had a hole in his chin?"

"I saw the movie. He acted like you, too."

"Yes, I suppose he was another such sullen brute as I."

"I love you better than anything in the world," I told him.

"Better than your daddy?"

I pretended to spit. I hoped he was going to say he loved me best, too, but all he said, rather pleased, was, "Well, Sinbad, you certainly know how to pick them."

The paper doll was my first unwilling acquaintance with Jem. One weekend my parents were staying in Washington with the Chasms. Jem, then about ten, presented my mother with a paper doll.

"There, you may have this one because it resembles you."

It was a dead-white Carmen with harsh eyebrows and flailing arms. For costume he had pailletted a scrap of black lace into a flamenco skirt with an underside of fuchsia satin, and secured her mantilla with pearl-headed pins. More of a voo-doo doll than a plaything, that Carmen was, with her severe expression, demented limbs, and pins sticking out of her. And indeed she turned out to be an instrument of torture not to me alone, for Mrs. Bocanegra Chasm was so enraged by the present she didn't speak to my mother that night.

"Carmen is *I*, darling," she remonstrated with Jem. "Mrs. Western does not have that heart-shaped face—*I* do."

"No," said Jem. "The Carmen is hers."

Mummy was enraptured, and on their return the stiff cray-oned figure was impaled by one of her pearl pins to the kitchen wall.

And so I loathed Jem before we met, because my mother, shaking her head, said darkly, "That boy is something else again."

"Yes, a troublemaker," said my father, who hadn't been im-pressed.

(Many years later I pointed out to Jem the paper doll who still seemed to be spitting at the company. He regarded her out of the corner of his eye: an animal playing unaware of the approaching enemy.

("Well, well. *Carmen est très maigre*," he said only, and went back to his book. But a moment later Jem said, "The right leg is too thin." And he set the doll on fire with the kitchen matches before I could intervene.

("Carmens should always go up in flames when nobody is willing to stab them.")

A few years after my own parents split up, I remember hearing that Mrs. Chasm had finally died in Mexico, and that Professor Chasm had taken the two boys back to England with him, where he had been offered a fellowship at All Souls. I hadn't thought of Professor Chasm for many years and on con-sideration no longer wished him to be mine alone, yet I was seized with a storm of jealousy at the thought of the care he was paying these boys without a mother, and this resentment was stirred again from time to time by reports that came back to me from my father in England.

These boys lived free as pirates and went traipsing about Spain and Italy on their mother's money, and my suspicions about the prosperity of sinners was confirmed when I heard that Jem had won himself a scholarship to Oxford. As for me, I was fifteen by then and had no desire even to finish high school, but I didn't want anyone else to, either.

Two

~~~

"Jezebel," said the boy. "What kind of malediction is *that?*"
He spoke in a dead-flat lisp, half American, half Continental
Drift. Given the extent to which the Chasm children were
embedded in my childhood's mythology, I was surprised that
he did not know my name. We had met only once before, on
a trip to the zoo, but the meeting had stuck in my mind. "We
met in an aviary," I told him.

"I know."

He was sitting on a black and white parquet floor, arranging cards in a circle around him. The upstairs drawing room
of the house in North Oxford was a burial chamber of treasure
and trash. There was a wooden Buddha peeling gilt, big as
King Kong but sedated; a vast seventeenth-century tapestry of
Aeneas's fleet in the port of Carthage; a classroom globe of the
world spinning turquoise, crimson, yellow; a green satin
chaise longue swathed in fur throws like a Russian sleigh. And
a rickshaw full of skeletons: a Mexican papier-mâché skeleton
in purple robes; an ivory and jewel-eyed Oriental death's head
(ideograms chiseled along the cranium); a wooden anatomy-
class Billy Bones; a human skull.

Seated in the midst of this mausoleum was the boy who,

like invalids, looked at once childish and antiquely ravaged, at once sharpened and preserved. And although he must have been almost six feet three, he possessed that tormented exquisite look of a child tossing in a fever bed. He wore black. He had since their mother died. "Do you remember Casimir in the aviary, too? Which of us do you remember?" he asked. "Casimir thinks he's so memorable, so distinguished. Distinguished like a potato."

Casimir was cuddling me on the chaise longue. I didn't like to be touched, but he was such a handsome boy, and had a way of always pawing you that was like people who cannot bear to be alone at night. He made Asia claw me too—the parrot that hung to his shoulder. Verminous and bit your ear. A deaf dowager. Casimir defended my name by attacking their own. "I don't know that we came off any lighter. Casimir sounds like a pimp in white go-go boots, and as for you, if Mama had had her way, you would be Netzahualcoyotl. She was going through a burst of nationalism," he explained to me, "for a country she left at the earliest possible opportunity."

Jem reflected. "Not that I'm on the angels' roll of honor as it is. Remember Jemmy Button?"

Jemmy Button was a Tierra del Fuegan savage picked up and dandified by the captain of HMS *Beagle*. He became quite a ladies' man for a year or so, an oversized General Tom Thumb in kid gloves and button boots, but even meeting the Queen couldn't convert a heathen beyond reclaim. Eventually they sent him home to the glacier jungles with soup tureens and beaver hats and a shipload of white linen and a mandate to spread Christianity, but when Darwin sailed around a year later, he found his pet had taken a cannibal wife and reverted to savagery.

"I'm glad my namesake wouldn't be tamed," said Jem. "Darwin was a sanctimonious fraud."

Jem turned two cards face up, and I saw that they were not

regular playing cards but tarot. He had turned up a prancing fool and a tower in flames. "Extravagances and destruction." That seemed to satisfy him. "That is you, Casimir, and your young friend. You can play, Scarlet Whore, if you will stop fornicating with my brother on the sofa." It was not mumbo jumbo of dark strangers and oceans to cross, but a proper French card game, like bridge.

I had imagined that Casimir, with his parrot on his shoulder and his buccaneer looks and wandering fingers, would have had a girl in every port. But when the last of the late arctic light had fled and their dour Spanish housekeeper laid out dinner and vanished, Jem said, "Lupita isn't used to girls. You are lucky to get fed at all."

The house in Belbroughton Road was bland in those days in the late nineteen seventies, the addictions that sprang up in it benign. The Chasms stayed up all night bolting chocolate milk shakes and gambling, and the boys' bedrooms testified to a reassuring boyishness. Casimir's room was as romantically wholesome as if a bereaved mother had left her soldier's possessions intact: bunk bed lit by a swinging kerosene lamp, pin-ups of Ava Gardner, a bullfight, T. E. Lawrence in headdress. A stuffed iguana and innumerable pairs of boxing gloves, roller skates, a fencing mask. Blowups of his own flickery black-and-white photographs of building sites, bomb-shelled buildings.

But Jem's room had the reproachful bareness of someone ready at any moment to pack his things and go. Even the books piled vertically in a shaky avenue of pagodas looked as if they might walk at night, leaving behind them unpaid bills.

Casimir and I broke off the round to gulp down some cheese soufflé. Jem waited, watching us from the floor. It took my appetite away.

"Casimir, I have just dealt."

Casimir was twanging over and over one string of a jazz

mandolin, thumping it for percussion. He was teaching the parrot to sing the blues.

"I gambled on your love, baby. And got a losin' hand. I gambled on your love, baaaaay-beee . . ."

"Your go."

"Your ways keep changin' . . . like the shiftin' desert sand." He flung away a trump which mine outranked, and began to wail again.

"I thought I'd be your king, baby . . . and you could be my queen. . . ."

"Casimir, you might deal now. It's a new round," from between Jem's gritted teeth. Casimir dropped the cards, the mandolin, the parrot, and slung out a new hand, complaining in a Ray Charles wheeze: "But you took me for your joker 'cause I thought your deal was clean." He pulled my hair thoughtfully, trying to look over my shoulder. He reminded me of those girls who braided my hair to the back of my chair at school, while pretending to caress.

"Oh daggers, you could do with a few high-rankers."

I swiveled to look at his hand. "Same to you, boy."

"Jesus!" Jem exploded. "Has neither of you a *trace* of the politic in you? If everyone knows what everyone's got, where's the game?"

"But everybody doesn't," I ventured. "We don't know what you've got, and you don't know what we've got."

"Yes, he does," said Casimir. "That's the game. The deck is loaded."

It was the summer I was seventeen when Casimir found me. I had been shunted over to England to stay with my father. It was the first time I had left the eastern shores of America, and England was my New World, my box of delights, if only I could figure out how to pry it open. Daddy, having taken me on a round of country houses, was at a loss to entertain a skulking teenaged girl. He was of an age when he didn't expect to have to entertain anyone under sixty and without likely gain. When the dowagers of his acquaintance told me that I must meet their sons, the sons were sure to be older than Daddy and forgers or kleptomaniacs into the bargain.

One night we went to dinner at the Chasms' house. It was a slapdash Victorian family house, all half-timber and pearly chapel windows. The boys lived on the top two floors of the house. There was a fire escape by which they came and went as they pleased, and it seemed as if Chasm didn't lay eyes on them for weeks on end.

Professor Chasm had married again, an Englishwoman with a good heart, it was clear, but hair like wig hair and a pulpy face and strident whine. Her name was Stephanie. She had leftist leanings and Chasm derived too much satisfaction from baiting her. Otherwise, he was permanently out of sorts. He had yellowing jowls now and a sozzled liver and his diatribes against American military cowardice and English food attested to a sour old age. It was a relief when Casimir came in after dinner to borrow some money, lucklessly trusting to his father's sense of public shame—"Ask Mr. Western for a loan: he's the one who is rolling in dough."

So Casimir, left high and dry, stayed on to hold forth, as young boys will, with a good deal of enthusiasm and ignorance. "Talks like a U.N. session," complained his father. Casimir, who was a few months younger than I, had just failed his A-Levels for the second time, and until he deigned to pass them would be unable to get work as a bus conductor, so there was much merriment that evening about his prospects as a gold digger. I didn't like this talk, but Casimir took it well, seemingly accustomed to being considered the fool of the family. And he stole my heart, not with his babble, but with his long black curls and red mouth and raw bones.

Casimir was scheming to break into his trust fund. Over the last year his brother had beat him daily at games of fortune, lending Casimir sums he could never hope to repay. Casimir went up to London to buy crocodile skin shoes; he brought me white chocolate and pink champagne and took me out to Caribbean nightclubs in the suburbs, until he was too poor to buy peanuts at the Rose and Crown.

"You spend like a sailor on payday," said Jem. Jem was a skinflint; he lived on air. Casimir begged to have another chance to reverse the score, but Jem was going away. He was leaving for Spain to study under the Jesuits in Salamanca. He lent Casimir another thousand pounds, all his ready money.

"Christian soldiers don't need cash," he said.

Casimir bought an eggshell blue Citroën whose doors didn't open, and he brought me back to the house in Oxford where night after night, weekend upon weekend, I spent the night on the chaise longue. I fought tears of vexation when Jem wasn't home and was scared to be alone with him when he was.

When I first had laid eyes on Jem that summer I was turned to stone, and when I saw him again I was seized by a trembling crazy exaltation such as I had known only before God. It seemed to me mad and sinful, this love of Jem that was more like fear and scorn. Casimir couldn't care less which of them I fell for. He regarded people as a mine to be plundered, by Jem as much as by him, but Jem would not touch what was not his alone. He insulted me to Casimir, calling me the beautiful idiot, the airhead, until he could see his way to snatching me, and Casimir reported my progress in Jem's affections without malice. "He says you could be quite pretty in the most bucolic sort of way, if your mouth weren't always hanging open to your knees." He was humiliating me until I would think myself fit for nothing but to be reconstructed by him. And Casimir would not save me, not hang on to me, not even notice that I had slipped from his loose grasp.

I came to stay the weekend Jem was leaving for Salamanca. Lupita showed me upstairs into the room they called the ball-room. A grand waltz was making the parquet quaver like palm trees under a tropical storm, but only Jem was there, advancing toward me wrapped up in a fur throw. The open French windows were battering to and fro to a high wind, the waltz whirled toward a demoniacally gay crescendo. A low-budget Dracula. The fur blanket slipped as he bent to kiss me—that kiss on both sides which veered dangerously close to one's cheek, if Jem was feeling amiable—and Jem was only in a shrunken white nightshirt that did not reach his knees. Pretty, stalky child's legs. Oh, it was going to be a ritual, all right. The swinging censers and the white lawn and all. The last will and testament. The little cake with his mother's blessing or the big cake without.

"Casimir is still at a fencing lesson so I've got you to my own devices."

"Fine, as long as we don't gamble—I'm dead broke."

"And playing with chips is too dismal, don't you think?" Jem agreed.

I had had fantasies of playing blackjack with Jem. A future of Casimir and myself white slaves in his debt, and in death, the children inheriting a legacy of debts.

"Come have some tea. Lupita is taking her nap now, so it's the only hour we can ransack the kitchen." I followed. The kitchen was tiled like a swimming pool and smelled like scorched milk. It was the only warm room in the house, the only comfortable one (Jem's own arrangements allowed for no position between vertical and supine), but Lupita was like the "Beware of Dog" sign before a luscious garden. She knew no English, and although Professor Chasm and Jem spoke Spanish, Lupita was from the Basque coast and her accent was impenetrable. Even Mrs. Chasm had been unable to understand her. Jem insisted upon talking to her about Basque terrorism, although she had left Spain forty years ago with the Bocanegras and knew nothing of what had happened since, nor did she care. But Jem insisted she was a Communist, and when she simply turned her back on his talk he felt himself vindicated. "That is why she hates Asia so," he explained. "She regards pets as the parasites of parasites."

But Asia was the only living creature Lupita talked to: when Asia squawked and flapped her wings at her, Lupita squawked and flapped back, and she tried to pinch her when nobody was looking. Lupita's passion wasn't politics but money. She felt the Bocanegra fortune belonged to her and tried to fend off any encroachment upon it. She could just about tolerate the Professor because, scruffy as he was, she had seen him appear on television in America, but the boys she considered feckless and degenerate. And then there was the running battle between Lupita and Jem over who would do the marketing. Going to the market was the only event, the only outside contact of either Jem's or Lupita's life. Each wanted it for himself, for they couldn't go shopping together; Jem was too proud and scratchy with servants, and Lupita couldn't take her cut if Jem kept the household money. Why should the oldest son hanker after a charwoman's chore, Lupita wanted to know, and "What does she need all that money for?" Jem grumbled. "She never leaves the house. She has no friends. She can't drive. She doesn't visit Christ Church Gallery, or take classes at the Polytechnic, or go look at Blenheim. She just watches television. With the sound off."

Lupita made up the words to "The Avengers." Jem talked back to Erasmus for company.

Now he spoke to me with the stilted deliberation of people who have lived alone too long and become accustomed to polishing their words in their head, rubbing them together like sea stones.

He sat me down on a high stool and slapped down before me bread and butter, a jar of black olive paste, a pot of gunpowder tea. He stood and watched. "Why aren't you eating?" he accused me. "You're not one of those Americans that doesn't like anything foreign but deep-freeze Brie?" He poured the tea. "Look," he said appealingly, "each bud explodes. That's why it's gunpowder."

"I don't like to eat in front of strangers," I said. "Why aren't *you* eating, anyway?"

He smiled. "I don't either."

That established, we polished off the bread and black paste. But Jem now seemed determined to outdo me in nicety. He held a fork by the tip of its handle and stared at the morsel at length, at last lifting it to a mouth opened like a bird waiting for its worm. If I spoke before the spiked mouthful had reached his mouth, it descended to the plate until we were silent again. It was something of a conversation stopper. He was a forbidding prospect anyway.

If you asked him a question he answered with a question: "Why? Why do you want to know?"

His shyness was tricky and defensive and there was much one couldn't mention: his dead mother for whom he was still in mourning, his father and stepmother whom he couldn't bear; his past was closed, and as for his present pursuits, like many English boys he made great show of doing nothing effortlessly—he picked flowers and drew pictures, as far as I could see, and carried about books in his pockets which he read in the bath and on the tops of buses. As for his future, the thought made him skittish with fear and resentment. There was some talk of his becoming a writer, a calling consonant with doing nothing and carrying about unread books. Casimir had shown me a sonnet that boded ill: a flawless construction on a mythological theme: Dido and Aeneas, like the tapestry, but it was an exercise in domination, an impatient intellect reducing emotion to a little gasp, a boa constrictor squeezing itself to death. And as for Salamanca, who knew why he was leaving university with only a year to go, and how he had come to be in the Jesuits' thrall?

There is a scary delight in trespassing on forbidden topics. I didn't possess the requisite unconcern—Casimir, for instance, could ask rude questions as if he weren't even intending to listen to the answers—but I asked nevertheless. Had he a calling?

Jem went rigid, began pushing his food about on the plate, eating off mine. "A calling for what?" he demanded, and after much resistance explained grudgingly that there was a priest at the university who was a patristics scholar and Jem wanted to study under him.

"So you don't even believe?" I said accusingly. Was it true, as Casimir had told me, that the fathers themselves were all atheists today?

Jem was impatient. "Don't be so damned earnest, Jezebel. Jesuitry means one doesn't question the rules of the game: one plays. What about you, Scarlet? What do *you* believe? What do *you* play? Did God put you on the face of this earth to pout and gape and suck your dirty thumb? How do you account for this losing hand of a life? I bet you think you're chosen, don't you? God's no-'count, do-nothing chosen. And the rest of us initiate and labor and maintain and scheme, while God's useless chosen sit on their porch gliders gazing with those glassy pale blue eyes like rocking horse eyes." He was glaring into my pale blue eyes now, Jem who rarely looked at anyone straight, and he pulled a face, as one might make a face at oneself in the mirror, not liking what one saw.

When Casimir came home we were ignoring each other over the rims of our glasses of green tea.

Casimir that year had been taken up in a big way by under-graduates and dons and those aging misfits who hang around university towns on money from home. Casimir enjoyed the fuss made of him, and, like any accomplished coquette, while seeming to lavish all, he withheld everything. Except for gossip. He had the biggest mouth I ever encountered. About his own affairs, he lied through his teeth; you could tell when he was lying from a trick of pursing up his lips in a particularly arch, cherubic pucker when something especially untrue was about to sully them. But about his family he told everything he had ever heard, always adding, "Don't tell Jem: he'd slit my throat for telling you. Remember, I'm your goose with golden eggs."

His seeming insensibility meant that people had always talked before him as if he weren't there, and Casimir had profited from it by memorizing everything said before him and filling in the significant blanks.

The element of untruth was like the alloy in a precious metal. Each batch had its unmistakable impurity, but the proportion was incalculable, and the ingredient different each time. I waited for him to come up with a real whopper: Jem and the Barbary pirates, Jem breaks the bank at Monte Carlo. But Casimir never slipped so much that one could pick out the strand of untruth. I called him Cholly Knickerbocker.

"You should make your disclosures lucrative."

He held out his palm expectantly.

At first I thought Casimir was just an uncommon blabbermouth, but gradually I saw that he had Jem on the brain no less than I did, an obsession half-reverent, half-obscene, and unexpected in a boy himself adventurous. And that his seeming generosity in relinquishing me to Jem was really just that he found more interesting what Jem would do with me than what he could.

What I knew of Casimir's many lives at Oxford was at odds

with this vicariousness. He was callous and exploitative; his nights were spent between going to high table and the opera with fidgety dons who tried to hold his hand, and undergraduate dinners where furniture was thrown through chapel windows and statues disfigured. He took me with him everywhere women were reviled and Americans unwelcome. But I never liked seeing people drunk, and Oxford that summer seemed to be swimming in a sea of Famous Grouse and flat soda. That night Casimir was going on to the King's Arms to meet an Australian photographer with some stunners of Russian tanks in the snow. He wanted me to come. Casimir wanted to be a photographer himself, a war correspondent.

"She can stay with me and pack," said Jem.

Casimir stuck out his lower lip and shrugged. "*Your* last night." And so I sat on the floor of the ballroom while Jem dragged all his possessions into the room and deposited them at my feet, as lionesses do. He wanted to give me everything: all his black leather motorcycle jackets and black drainpipe trousers and black T-shirts.

"What do I want all this for? I'm not planning to join the resistance," I objected.

Jem wanted to dispose of all his worldly trappings. Even the suitcase—a gnawed canvas valise splattered with other people's voyages—was to be empty. I refused most of what he offered me. I didn't want him to be my cult. And as it goes with those who decline, the stakes grew higher. From offering me ratty black pullovers, Jem rose to his grandfather's pocket watch, his mother's diamond shoe buckles. No. I dug my heels into the ground.

"Immaculata," he sighed. "Your price is high."

"You used to call me Scarlet Whore."

"I didn't know you very well."

He swept in and out of the ballroom in a cloud of white

nightgown, reappearing with armloads of photographs and magazines conjured up from under the bed or floorboards of an empty room. He dropped at my feet a pile of Iranian broadsheets from the past couple of months. "See the record of God's chosen, who work upon choice more assiduously than you." I couldn't read the words, but the caricatured effigies screamed across their victims. "God's chosen utter more tripe than *China Reconstructs*," said Jem. He wanted to give me all his books, his records, even the drawing room furniture.

"Take a ship back to America," he urged. "Get yourself a cabin on a Russian freighter, and you can sit in it like a songbird in an overstuffed cage."

He came out of his bedroom once more with a last load of books. A pile for Casimir—even brash, ignorant gigolo Casimir, his sometime enemy, got the *Arabian Nights*, Richard Burton's version with its racy preface. Ritual had swept all his jealousies away. A scattering for himself, to weigh down his few black suits like pennies on a dead man's eyes. And for me, he dropped at my feet that jeweled Chrysostom, Bishop Taylor.

Jeremy Taylor was a Catholic suspect, Jem explained, friend to Laud and Charles I, who for unknown reasons was never recalled from banishment during the Restoration, but pined in Ireland like Ovid among the Goths. A Victorian forerunner smack in the middle of the seventeenth century, closer to Ruskin in syntax and sentiment than to the Royal Society.

"*Holy Living and Holy Dying*—that just about covers it," I said.

"That is for humility. God's chosen—we'll see," he said grimly. "I'll look out for you on Judgment Day to see who picks you for his team. Anyway, I suppose you only read *The Great Gatsby* at school. Listen. 'Here is no place to sit down in, but you must rise as soon as you are set, for we have gnats in our chambers, and worms in our gardens, and spiders and flies in the palaces of the greatest kings. . . . Grand Cairo in Egypt feels the plague every three years returning like a quartan ague, and destroying many thousands of persons. All the inhabitants of Arabia the desert are in continual fear of being buried in huge heaps of sand, and therefore dwell in tents and ambulatory houses, or retire to unfruitful mountains, to prolong an uneasy and wilder life.' "

Oh, these long long lives we lead have turned us into gelded beasts, to chewed cud. Then the living were the quick, and now they are laid back. I have *Holy Living and Holy Dying* still, and veering across the flyleaf, in an emerald green, angular hand, "Jezebel from NJC, Oxford July 1978." That night I held the book fresh from his hands and knew that I would be living off the hope of any scent of Jem that clung to its leaves: a scent of black tobacco and starched cotton and steamed milk. It went to my head, knowing that I would have to feed—for how many months?—off the recollection of what was now the present moment. It made me restless to push him off so I could start dreaming about him.

Jem was jittery that night. "Can you dance?" he asked. "I don't mean wiggle your hips—can you waltz? It's a thrill like a mad horse under you, a quick spirited waltz like this. I like dancing where you must keep your eyes open."

He took hold of me at a clenched arm's length until the music got high-flown again and cantered away with me. I tried to think of the champagne and the pink sky and the boys in black in Eustacius's bedtime stories, but I clung and flopped about. I stomped on his bare feet. Jem halted. "Now, look here, who is leading? If you're not a boy, don't lead. If you can't waltz, don't lead. You *melt*."

That ferocious gravelly voice ordered me to melt into his bony bosom. That most vertical tin soldier accused me of being stiff. I gave him a really sarcastic, mutinous waltz. And once more Jem stalled and said sweetly, "I know all too well what an affront it is to be told to relax. But the dance floor is not a boxing ring, so stop treading on me and bruising my shoulder, and *do* as I *do*."

"It's not the Spanish Riding School, either."

Jem flopped down at my feet and tugged me down beside him. Now for a quick, spirited conversation? With our eyes open? Jem never laughed and I never smiled. His smile was one twist of his crooked mouth way to one side of his face. I could poker-stare him into discomfort. It's a sad world and you take up the habit of twisting your pains into jests; a twist of the mind that becomes a constitutional tic. I never bothered, and Jem just plain didn't think it was funny. He finished packing in silence and then he said, "I would rather you not mess around with Casimir."

"But I don't."

"Why? Is he no good in bed?" A sudden sparkle of happy malice struck him.

"Oh, get lost. Go to Salamanca. Go to bed. You're too presumptuous."

But Jem didn't go to bed. The next morning when I woke up the green satin chaise longue was piled high with white tulips for me.

"He's at it again," said Casimir darkly.

"At what?"

"Breaking into the Botanical Gardens. It *is* naughty of him. They've got a great hulking Alsatian loose there, to keep vandals out of the greenhouses at night. I should have snatched the orchids if I were going to all the trouble, but he is such an intolerable purist."

Over breakfast, Jem scowled an acknowledgment. "Oh, well, those frozen tulips they fly in from Holland are nasty.

They melt to ashes in the bud, and spare you the delight of watching them burst open and drop, petal by petal."

"Jemmy, I'll dance with you whenever you like," volunteered Casimir. "And I promise not to lead. But I want orchids."

Three

I had one friend back at school in New York: the Spanish teacher. This man was dogmatic and bad-tempered, one of those ardent Communists who have their shoes made in Italy. We fought and ridiculed each other but we shared one great loathing—school—so we got along. We lunched together every day in the cafeteria along a balcony overlooking the gym, and I cut sports every afternoon to walk with him along the pier overlooking the East River. He called me La Fanciulla del West. When my father, who was in New York for a sale at Christie's and feeling proprietary, wanted to know whether I was getting along any better, I mentioned the teacher I liked.

"That doesn't sound very suitable."

"Well, suitable is a difficult word, Daddy, and relative. He wouldn't suit you, but he does suit me."

"What about Marshall's daughter? Why don't you take her up? She seems like a sensible enough girl."

"Daddy, that girl is about five years old. They've put her to bed by the time I even get to school."

Then the Spanish teacher started waiting for me on my doorstep in the mornings and seeing me home in the afternoon. I made vicious fun of him. My mother thought he was cute.

At a parents/teachers cocktail party my father asked him, jocularly, "Is Jezebel a good student?"

"A student. Not a good student at all, no," said the Spanish teacher, too seriously. "She is rather an Undine, who drags down the scholars around her to the depths of her world. It is not malice—with such a spirit she could not do otherwise."

Daddy did not like this much. It sounded delightful, but rather dangerous. What were my chances of getting into a decent university?

The teacher got angry. *Must* I go to school and school and school like every hack? *Must* I have a career, like the mundane? Would my father be the wreck of me altogether?

Daddy, in one of those sweeps of the board which turned him from squeaking cherub to decorous affronted, asked what Senor Comacho y Ibarra would suggest as an alternative.

There was a casino in Macao where lady croupiers in dinner jackets and diamond studs leveled loaded pistols at unruly customers. . . . My father thought I should be removed from this school. My mother thought it was sort of sweet that the teacher had a crush on me—he couldn't be much more than thirty.

"A crush on her? He said she was only fit to be a nightclub bouncer." I stayed on, but I was so exasperated by the Spanish teacher's stupidity, his breach of conduct, that I did not speak to him again. I stared right through him during class, except when whispering to my neighbors; his violent trembling, his dropping books and breaking chalk were a reward for learning girl talk. He would snarl, "Silence!" But he never called on me any more. He followed me after school when I chose to be walking with new companions, laughing and swinging my books.

One afternoon I dropped my Spanish book deliberately

and did not pick it up. The next morning in class, when we were asked questions on the homework, he addressed me for the first time.

"Senorita Western. *¿Qué está en el cofre del Cid?*"

I leaned my chair back on its hind legs and gazed at the ceiling. "*El Cid.*"

My smarmy classmates giggled but he quieted them.

"Senorita Western, *otra vez. ¿Qué está en el cofre del Cid?*"

It was the kind of question he himself found too boring to live.

"Oh, a mess of silver and gold, I expect."

"Senorita Western, perhaps you would find it easier to answer me if you had your book." He spoke correct English when he was angry. "Have you lost it?" he asked.

"No, I have it."

He came down the aisle then and handed my schoolbook to me. On the flyleaf was written, as I knew there would be, in a governessy copperplate, "Dropped and scorned like this book, but still, my life's blood, I have not forgotten you," it began. When class was over I eased the book off the desk until it fell with a bang, and walked out.

The next day he drew me up against the lockers and told me, "This school is not big enough for the two of us." With his twirled mustachios and his heavy accent tickling me, he sounded like the desperado in a one-horse town. La Fanciulla stayed.

I still have somewhere a volume of St. John of the Cross inscribed, "To my little demon in the fond hopes that she never compromise as has her servant, Joachim Comacho y Ibarra."

Now I had sudden side equal to that of girls with important parents or expensive jewelry. Everyone thought that I had been to bed with the Spanish teacher and that my father had gotten the man sacked for it, but I had been too long a class creep to trust to the illumination. I enjoyed, too uneasily, the month or so during which the smart girls copied my odd accent and threadbare clothes, affected an interest in God and vengeance, but when the bolder ones pressed for details of the Spanish teacher's prowess, I said, "Search me—I barely knew the man." They lost interest, but I kept a few more pliable creatures to bend to my will. I liked to hear from clean mouths my foul expressions. Men on the street had begun to follow me home, my parents' friends looked at me askance. I made myself all curves of suggestion, promises to be fleshed out, and aesthetes with good sense said there was trouble to come.

When I was younger I had stayed home, listening to Mummy's and Eustacius's stories until Mummy could no longer reproach herself for not having given me a proper childhood, for she had made over to me the deed to her own, which, if not quite proper, was full-blooded enough. I moved about in this house of lives until I came to inhabit it, and it suited me more than my own. My own life had always had to me the air of large empty rooms with packing cases in them, lumber rooms; I always felt as if I were sitting on one of the packing cases, unwilling either to move on or to unpack my possessions. You can live a whole life like that, without un-packing your soul or setting up house in your body, and it is a solitary kind of frittering. After I met Jem this inherited pack of lives was no longer enough for me. I knew my own life was somewhere else, wrapped up in his, so I kept my waking days bare and wooden; but the nights were ebony, ivory, gold, and I dreamed of Jem. I waited out my last two years of school, cutting dead even my few jerky school friends—I didn't want friends. Waiting for Jem, whose gruesome beauty was a hum in my blood. Carving his name on my school desk, deeper and deeper, increasingly irritated by all the sounds and smells that distracted me from him. Objecting, in cultivated tones, to the way Mummy picked food from the platter with her fingers and wore the same pair of blue jeans day in, day out, because she liked them best.

"I wouldn't fret so if I could help it, sugar pie," she said sympathetically, as if her discarded clothes on the living room floor were a circumstance beyond anyone's control.

In the late spring of my senior year, she went out to an ashram in Colorado for a couple of months and Daddy came over from London to look after me. The house got very clean and Eustacius stayed in the kitchen where he belonged. Daddy tried to get me interested in arranging flowers and linen cupboards. When I came downstairs in the morning he checked to see that I was carrying a handkerchief and that my shoes had been polished. I kept my Puerto Rican boyfriends out of the house. That summer Daddy took me to a grand place in Haiti. The Chasms seemed farther away than stars in the sky. Jem would perhaps be already ordained, already canonized. I knew that I would never have him the way I wanted him.

It was the next Christmas when Casimir came to America for college interviews. He had scraped through A-Levels so narrowly that he expected no decent English university would take him. Professor Chasm petitioned all his American cronies to squeeze Casimir in somewhere. Casimir swooped down on our house between interviews, teased Eustacius, flirted with Mummy, and took me ice-skating.

The rink at Rockefeller Center was a charmed circle of old ladies in candy pink tutus and guttersnipes plastered to the barriers, shrieking encouragement.

"Go 'way, nasty little boys," shrilled a candy-floss foxtrotter. Her partner waggled a threatening mitten at the spectators catcalling them. A little girl bumped into the princess of the rink and the lady gave the child a hard push. "If you can't skate, little girl, you'll have to leave the rink."

Casimir did not like this. He had been spinning me around the ring at top speed, ignoring the tinkled dance measures, but now he let me go and played grappling beginner. With mounting speed and flailing arms, Casimir cannonballed into the princess in tutu, clutching at her for support, and almost bringing them both down in a football tackle.

The onlooking gang of children howled with glee. Casimir and I were asked to leave the rink: falling down was against the rules. We walked up Fifth Avenue in the falling twilight mixed with snow. Two Salvation Army Santa Clauses were coming to blows over a street corner each claimed as his own. Casimir was mauled and buffeted by ladies maddened by his stargazer pace. We paused before the Grand Army Plaza lineup of nags festooned in flowers, considering a carriage ride around the park, while the owners screamed allurements at us. We cruised up and down the rows of park benches where black boys sell every pill in the *Physician's Desk Reference*, but the park was deserted in the dark. We crossed the street to the Prague for hot chocolate. A molting waiter stuck us in a corner banquette whose mustard velvet was worn down to the bone.

That first meeting with Jem and Casimir, more than half a dozen years before, was my only meeting with Mrs. Chasm. Although our fathers were inseparable, children, even in those liberal days, met only if their nannies frequented the same park. Past avenues of cages, with very quick, tiny steps on tottery heels, a lady in a tailored midnight-blue suit, with blue-black hair coiled high. Behind, two overgrown malcontents who looked about to snatch her midnight-blue crocodile handbag.

It was an expedition to the new aviary at the zoo for the

benefit of introducing us and, as those arrangements tend to go, loftily unsuccessful. No one, including Mrs. Chasm, gave a damn for birds. Jem, Casimir, and I were somewhere from ten to twelve and too old to appreciate being taken to the zoo. I had expected the Professor to be there, and sulked; Casimir and Jem were sulking too, for reasons known only to their mother.

Jem once told me that we are each born with an animal self, and I suppose people go to the zoo for some awful joke upon themselves. Mrs. Chasm's tour of the animals was a beauty pageant. The caged jaguars and cheetahs she regarded askance—that was *her* joke, and she didn't like it one bit. The reptiles scored well; the flamingos were moth-eaten, but she liked their stalky legs. The rhinoceroses and hippopotami were no better than pigs.

I remember now Mrs. Chasm coaxing Jem: "Look, my heart's darling, look at the marvelous elephant. Isn't it ridiculously fat?" while Jem turned his back. Jem emptied his bag of peanuts into a baby carriage rather than let either Casimir or the elephant have it.

I am told we went afterwards for tea at the Prague, but I don't remember that.

What sticks in the memory was Jem, when asked if he had enjoyed the afternoon, replying, with a Spanish accent: "The devil I did. The monkey house *stank*."

"Jem would devour this place," said Casimir. "It's his staple diet: hot chocolate and petits fours. He's got the habits of a Pekingese." I pushed an éclair around my plate sporadically before asking, "Well, what's become of Jem anyway? Is he a saint yet?"

"It's rather hard to tell, Jem not being the confiding kind. He's been back in Oxford six months now, moping and cursing and teaching me to throw knives. He was studying Russian for a while, but seems to have abandoned it."

"He had a good time in Spain?"

"Well, Jem's good times," Casimir said darkly. "Although he would preach to one no end about the importance of having a good time, that doesn't mean he's obliged to go in for them himself. He seems to have left the Jesuits under rather a cloud. Jem, as you know, has got this hunger for making everyone his slave of love. Me, I just try to get laid, but Jem goes in for this very spiritual, worshipful love, and this time he seems to have dragged the entire college of saints into his love nest. Except that everything always ends in tears. I went over to see him for the Semana Santa, and I can tell you I've never seen such a spectacle. Jemmy could scarcely go out for a cup of coffee without a convoy of priests buzzing about the honey pot—I mean, it was like Richard III if one tried to have a word with him, prayerbook in hand and a bishop on either elbow and 'O do not swear, my lord of Buckingham'—Jem the foulest-mouthed boy on the block. So what went wrong? Search me. All I know is what I'm told. That for a year or so Jemmy was the unrevealed miracle worker of the fathers, and then he came storming home with an uncommonly mean look in his eye.

"Now, some people when they lose religion, hit the bottle, but Jem hit society. He's become a tremendous beau."

I tried to envisage Jem a pomaded gallant, but Casimir assured me that he was still as knock-kneed and grueling as ever. He had simply spread his nets as if unconscious of the fish that swam in. There was a taggle of druggy heiresses now screaming in pursuit. "Your chaise longue is now much in demand. There's always at least one rich runaway stowed in the ballroom," complained Casimir.

"I can't imagine that he'd like that much," I said sourly, riveted by jealousy.

"Oh, you know, he pretends to be such a tyrant and the idea is that these floozies keep the place spotless. . . . But the truth is that Jem's discovered girls at the great age of twenty and hasn't yet figured out what to do with them, so he asks them back to the house at night and then tells them to wash the floors and take out the trash. Now you know what a maniacal housekeeper the boy is himself. His stomach turns at the sight of crumpled sheets or a dirty ashtray. He'd have fired Lupita if she hadn't left of her own accord. Didn't you know? She's gone back to Spain. I was petrified that she was going to die on us. Jem thinks she's gone to lead the Basque Separatists. *Well.* She'll be the richest lady in Zuroao—she's gone to play grande dame.

"The debutantes. Well, the last time I was at the house there was a fuchsia-lipped girl in a turquoise New Look dress with rosebudded stilettos dusting—well, violently shifting the dust from one corner to another. She did not look very happy. She said she was going home. She had thought that she had been badly treated *there*, but she'd never had to sweep floors. I wouldn't mind about the girls," Casimir concluded, "but he won't go to bed with them, and he won't let me either."

The éclair came in for some more mauling. Jem was charmless. He looked like a child with rickets; the thin greenish arms riddled with scars, the stalk legs, a face dominated by a great bee-stung mouth (crooked), eyes murky circular pools with leaden lids, the flattened nose. I hated his guts. Always had. That articulated whisper. That lisping snarl. Those sweet insulting things you thought he had never said before. He probably called them all airheads and scarlet whores. He was a sort of mutant, he was dull and pompous. The éclair rolled onto its stomach at a last stab.

But that wasn't the end of it. In bars along Third Avenue Casimir told me what had replaced Jesuits and debutantes in Jem's attentions. A family called Shaw. The husband was a

banker, the wife an alcoholic Pole. One of the daughters Jem
had chosen from the chain gang of that year's debutantes: a
real *jeune fille bien élevée*, not very pretty, very correct. Not
used to the attention. And he had mesmerized the entire family, at first grateful, then transfixed. A grand house to stay in
in London, a mess of servants (but Jem never knew how to
talk to servants), a steady flux of provocative company. But he
liked families only when they were pitted against one another,
and so, if dreamily, he dropped the daughters, ignored Mr.
Shaw, and focused upon Mrs. Shaw. He sat at her feet and
looked into her eyes as he talked. Then she seemed to go over
the edge. When he didn't come to London, Mrs. Shaw was
driven to Oxford, where she stood outside the house all night
long, wrapped up in a sable coat. Jem got very hysterical about
it all, and refused to leave the house or even look out the
window. All he would do was demand every five minutes that
Casimir go look if she was still there. "Really," said Casimir,
"he was more of a goose than she. There was a don Jem was
very secretive about—well, you and I know Jem is secretive
about the *lamppost*—but she was convinced that Jem was
sleeping with this don. Well, he always used to go around to
see the man late at night and stay till dawn, so of course she
thought the worst. Even though he was about eighty. Europeans think sex is behind everything."

Mrs. Shaw put a detective on Jem. The detective had mistaken Casimir for Jem and followed him to the King's Arms
and the cinema. He picked an especially existential film to
bore the man, and then made out with his girl friend of the
time all the way through it. Afterwards he had gotten into a
punchout with the detective, and had his nose broken for the
third but not last time. When he got home, Jem swabbed it
with brutal efficiency. "I wish you would let me set it for you,"
he had said. "I may not get another chance for ages, and
you've not got much to lose." Casimir was fed up. "If you

4 1

don't go talk to that lady downstairs, I'll give *you* a broken nose to set."

Jem had preened a bit about how it was too embarrassing, he couldn't possibly, the woman could sit on the pavement if she liked, it would be presumptuous to talk to her, she wouldn't like it; anyway, he didn't feel like it, what business was it of his where she spent her nights. Casimir forced him down the stairs and into the street, without a jacket or overcoat. The woman in sable coat and dark glasses didn't look at him. Jem leaned against the railings and gazed at her off and on for what seemed like ages before going over to her.

"Won't you come upstairs, Mrs. Shaw?" he asked coaxingly, and when she didn't answer took her by both hands. "For God's sake, do come on." She didn't answer.

"Why are you sleeping with that ugly old man?" she said at last.

Jem dropped her hands and went back inside, reappearing an instant later with a bottle of vodka. He sat down on the steps and gestured that she sit beside him.

"Why, my poor child, you are cold as ice," Mrs. Shaw said at last, wrapping her coat around the two of them. Jem leaned against her, his head almost against her shoulder, and so they sat on the frozen steps until dawn, taking swigs from the bottle in turn, like Arctic mariners trying to keep the blood circulating.

"And not speaking?" I asked scornfully.

"Oh no—they kept me up all night, laughing and talking under my window, like a couple of tramps, for God's sake." Casimir may have been kept awake, but Mrs. Shaw's children found themselves homeless whenever Jem was over. Any previous acquaintance with the daughter was ignored. Mrs. Shaw simply sighed, "It's a pity that Jem doesn't like Geoffrey or the children."

"I should think Mr. Shaw would like to see Jem iced."

"Are you joking? This is *England*. The man couldn't care less so long as his wife is *fairly* circumspect. And it keeps her off the bottle, more or less."

"What is she like, anyway?"

"Ardent and innocent, says tremendously funny things, and one can't tell whether they are meant to be funny or not. She's a woman to have your nose knocked sideways for."

"You sound besotted with her yourself," I said, exasperated.

"I would *die* for that goose."

The ink-blue car and chauffeur drove Jem to and from London every week; her husband was obliged to take the underground. Mrs. Shaw accompanied Jem everywhere, and his tyrannical courtliness made her presence seem a graceful acquiescence and not just tagging along. He took her to late-night films with Casimir and his scruffy friends, and to penny arcades, where she hit the jackpot and made the pinball machines sing.

"You're lucky tonight, Mrs. Shaw." Casimir would beam, trying to be kind.

"Mrs. Shaw is always lucky," said Jem.

He propelled her gently by an arm around her waist, and as soon as she wilted he felt it at his fingertips and bent over to inquire, "Shall I take you home, Mrs. Shaw, or are you still amused by the riffraff?"

She didn't listen to his talk. She didn't cosset him. She watched, and she saw. She told Jem something that he never divulged, although it changed him: what lay in the future for him. She understood the fear that was clogging his confusing gifts, that kept him restless and idle. She drew people to her house who would rouse him, and after everyone left, Jem and Mrs. Shaw sat up all night swilling vodka. I boiled to think of Jem with his Pro Keds on the lacquered tables, stroking the kid of her gloved hand and talking to her of Bishop Taylor and the Church Fathers. She understood, too, how easily he tired, and how exhaustion made him see blackness.

When he was still gesticulating fractiously in a too bright flash, a last gasp that seemed like second wind, she led him forcibly to his new quarters, where her mother had used to live: a rajah's suite, all orchids and elephant tusks, a carved, entwined fourposter bedstead swathed in flaming brocades and taffy-colored fur blankets.

"There is the inside telephone. Ring when you want something," said Mrs. Shaw, and left him.

I could see him lying rigidly across the bed, his eyes wide open and staring into the dark, until they guttered.

Four

Things don't get interesting until you see the pattern connecting them. Mrs. Shaw is just the Polish goose until you place her in the scheme: a calmer, fitter-for-survival counterpoint to Mrs. Chasm, an Odette to her Odile.

There must be a Day of Judgment on which to stand up such soul destroyers, who concoct a labyrinth of intrigue, blossoming on lies and crocodile tears, a labyrinth in which husbands get entangled, children lost, strangers helplessly implicated. A Doomsday on which to stand up such wreckers and return the slaps they deal out so lavishly. But St. Michael doesn't sound like a face slapper: piff-paff, the palm and the back.

Perhaps her torments were enough as Senorita Bocanegra de la Igaron, too tall, too proud, too pale. Storming in a ranch in the pine mountains of Chiapas, almost at the Guatemala border, while her father got richer. Green hell, those gracious haciendas must have been. They looked charmed enough to the Bostonians and Europeans stopping by for the weekend: the dance got up for their pleasure, the peons strumming quavery sad songs, slumped in a doorway. The seigneur was a gay raconteur if you hadn't heard the stories before. Everything for the English gentleman, anything for the foreign visitors. Whose horse is that? Why, it is yours. Everything except for the daughters, who, like smoldering Dians, didn't appear.

Her father was a Royalist who had come to Mexico at the start of the Spanish Civil War, an import-exporter who worked in Vera Cruz and in Mexico City, which he thought too fast for unmarried women. So the daughters pined in the mountains. Those black eyebrows would grow together from too much frowning, they were told. Let them. Who was there to see? Born in Mexico, except for Ifigenia, they were taught to consider themselves Castilian and lisped and hissed a language incomprehensible to the servants.

If Mexico City was barred to them, there was always Vera Cruz in which to while away a season. Hot, sticky-sweet, disease-infested port, expiring into candy-colored shantytowns sucking the delta like leeches. Mornings of long-drawn-out visits among the ladies of the Spanish enclave, sitting poker-upright in stark drawing rooms admiring parakeets and puffy, sallow children.

A young lady could not linger about the docks, watching the stevedores unloading ships from Denmark, Athens, Liberia.

Bocanegra extolled English travelers. They were so correct. You could spot them before they came down the gangplank, by their upright bearing. You could spot their battered Gladstone bags. Mexican luggage—even the grandest—was suspect, screamingly funny and a little frightening, as if the odd-colored leather could only be flayed human skins.

But the Englishmen were accompanied by English ladies. When Ofelia saw them, she wanted to spit in their eyes. Those sisters, mothers, wives in white. So damning was their sartorial awareness of being in the tropics, the farthest reaches of hemisphere; they practically wore mosquito netting for veils.

Her father knew them all, and was considered good fun.

Stir crazy from weeks aboard ship, and ahead of them a por-
tentous penetration of the dark continent, they were delighted
to accept his hospitality, these prospectors: his house in town,
with its fleet of servants, its fountains of brandy and port, its
lace-edged sheets, the estancia in Chiapas for a rougher weekend. But although Bocanegra *much* wished that his poor
motherless daughters learn that wonderful British manner
from Senor Campbell's wife and sister, when it came down to
returning favors, no one seemed to wish to take up the girls.
The imagined afternoon drives discussing Sir Walter Scott
never materialized. The ladies were indisposed. The altitude
gave them migraine. The Bocanegritas' cheetah graces were
left undisturbed. Back to the mountains: the pestilent Veracru-
cian climate did not suit the young. Desperation scales blank
walls, shoots down its own quails from heaven.

There came an Englishman without wife or sisters, without mother. He was an Oxford don and he could drink Bocanegra under the table.

Bocanegra came to call at his fleabag hotel the afternoon
after their first bout. The *mozo*, who looked seedy himself,
said protectively that Dr. Chasm was still asleep. Whereupon
shouts came from the bedroom.

"Damn fool! I'm *not* durmiendo! Idiot! Come in!"

Bocanegra came in to be received by a long, stark-white
young man who drew the bedclothes up to the lowest of the
staring ribs that proceeded down his hollow chest, and ordered
another pot of coffee and a shot of tequila.

Charles Chasm was traveling through Mexico and Central
America before taking a post at Duke University in North Carolina. Why would a gentleman of learning wish to come to
this forsaken continent? asked Bocanegra.

Chasm rubbed together thumb and middle finger. Loot.
Bocanegra shrugged, puffed out his lips. Naturally.

"Anyway, England is a shit-hole," said Chasm. "It's too

damned egalitarian. These pathetic days the United States, I believe, is the last bastion of bigotry."

But bigotry was a great evil, no?

"Oh my dear friend, I don't want to teach Appalachians Ortega y Gasset, I simply don't."

"Ah, you are secretly a democrat. I see that your little *mozo* is a friend of yours."

"Oh, the fellow is miraculous. We'll get drunk together, but I still think he's a monkey, and he thinks I'm a fool, and if he borrows my dinner jacket again he's sacked."

Here was a man who said what Bocanegra and the other Spaniards said among themselves of the Mexicans: monkeys. My God, the English were marvelous. But mystifying.

"My friend, you talk of shit-holes and what, then, are you doing in this outhouse? If you don't come to live in my house *today*, I will never speak with you again."

Chasm alone penetrated the purdah. He was introduced to Ifigenia, Ofelia, Consuelo, and the dejected maiden aunt who taught them to embroider and to pray. He came to stay in Chiapas. It was the monsoon season, when you were trapped in the stark, icy sitting room while outside exploded into fiery greens, flamboyant trees whose fingers clutched as you passed under, disgorging fountains of water upon you.

The doctor made himself at home not by adapting, but by disrupting the household. He christened the pristine drawing room with an avalanche of Tauchnitzes and tobacco pouches, he crawled out of bed at noon, drinking and talking his way through lunch, refusing not only soup, fish, beefsteak, and pudding but Bocanegra's prized Johnny Walker, for straight tequila.

"Or, better still, haven't you got any mescal about the house?"

Bocanegra was torn between the customary "¿Cómo no?" (Are there black panthers up in these forests?—How could it be otherwise? ¡*Cómo no!*) and the impropriety of the question. It was like asking if they kept any pig slop in the deep freeze.

"Possibly the servants keep some about," said Bocanegra stiffly, and sent his houseboy to the bedroom cupboard to bring out a bottle of mescal. But when Chasm had killed the bottle, Bocanegra told him, with a great roar of laughter, where it came from. In the late afternoon, whose graven law proclaimed that even the vaqueros crawl under the nearest maguey and sleep, Chasm would not retire. "I only just got up," he explained. He went riding with Ofelia, who was never sleepy, never hungry, always thirsty. They rode through pine forests and black ravines and jungly paths silted with black volcanic dust. Chasm jogged about in the saddle, pretending almost to be pitched off, to make her laugh. Ofelia gripped, imperious, erect. Both were daredevil riders, flaying their horses' barrel bellies with whirring fighting-cock spurs until the animals cleared ravines, stormed along precipices. They smoked her father's cigars and took slugs from Chasm's hip flask, replenishing it with pulque at tenants' shacks along the way. Ofelia had been drinking since she was twelve years old. There was a leaf you chewed, and nobody could tell.

Bocanegra believed that his sister accompanied them, but making the lady stay in her bedroom had been an easy transaction. She was frightened of large animals and fond of her siesta. "We'll say a Hail Mary for you," said Chasm.

"You demolish my horses, you corrupt my servants, you petrify my sister, but you bring the pink back into my daughter's cheeks," roared Bocanegra, squeezing the breath out of his friend.

Chasm had tried to corrupt Ofelia, too, once when he was helping her dismount, but she kicked him under his horse. And so they became friends, something novel to both of them. He told her things about the country in which she lived that somewhat reconciled Ofelia to it: about jaguar gods and astronomers' palaces. Chasm went on to Guatemala, but he swooped back on his way to Duke. "I reckon that it will only prove a larger shit-hole than Oxford, but I expect better service."

At Christmas, when the pilasters of colonial houses in the capital were festooned with neon reindeer and the Reforma was a racecourse of tinsel, Charles Chasm came back. Lank and irritable as ever, and delighted with the inanity of the Carolinas.

"All the families are older than God and more English than the Queen, and they've made me an assistant professor." He turned to Ofelia and said with a new formality, "You, senorita, would be satisfied with the hunting, however: all pink coats and Jorrocks."

He asked for her hand in marriage.

"Why do you want to do *that*?"

"Well, it sounds a bit forced to say that I *can't* live without you—rather, why bother to?"

"Well, I don't know, really," she considered. "You are so very thin and yellow—like a dog, really. What does my father say?"

A brief gesture. "What do you think he says? Now come on."

Having no choice in the matter, she dignified it with the illusion of choice, as if she had trouble deciding.

"Your face is very crooked indeed, and you have no eyebrows to speak of. But I suppose ugliness wears better than prettiness." Later, she looked at herself in the silver-scaled mirror upstairs and made as if to spit.

"White slave."

And then, stretching long, slender arms to the girl in the glass, "My poor white slave, you have been bought."

The Professor did not bother with long engagements. He did not bother with his own family: father a retired diplomat, failed poet, who lived with his wife in Eastbourne. Not as many ships to gaze at as in Vera Cruz, Charles told her.

The reckless competitive masculine tenor of their drinking camaraderie was at an end. One could not be friends with a husband. And Professor Chasm's formality disguised a new desperation for Ofelia which rendered him tongue-tied. Now that they were properly engaged they had to sit in the drawing room all day, while neighbors—the nearest lived forty miles away—came to congratulate. (Make sure it is your own padre who marries you, so you know that you are married for certain.) And stayed.

I wonder did the Professor ever get cold feet during those downpours at the hacienda of dark, chattering cousins, tiny, preserved great-grandmothers, descending upon them for a wedding that lasted five days, five nights. *¡Qué fiesta! ¡Qué splendor!*

Of course the Professor was captivating, the next best thing to Shirley Temple. Stayed up later than all the night creatures, outdrank even her Uncle Porfirio, and slept later than a boa constrictor—in spite of her cousin Petronilo's assertion that the Englishman would get up at six for a walk, before wanting something called elevenses: perhaps a steaming mess of kedgeree without which the bridegroom would feel incomplete.

"Balls," said Bocanegra. "He is one of us."

Chasm even suffered Don Anibal, who also had gone to Oxford, to exercise his Latin upon the Professor.

"Very rusty," apologized the old man.

"Latin doesn't age," Chasm replied.

His willingness to please and ignorance of custom, his furiously right-wing politics at a time when clever young men were Marxist, entertained the household. But I believe that he was enchanted, too—that, especially at the age of twenty-nine, having served his term as an academic hack, the long-drawn-out tropic gaieties spinning themselves out on a peak in the Chiapan highlands could not cloy his high spirits. And Ofelia was tantalizing. He called her Cleopatra now—Ophelia was too gossamer a heroine—and she called him Yellow Dog. Capricious ravishments: somber and stern, and then with one sweep of the eyes smothering him with caresses. If the luckless duenna—an aunt or a sister—interposed, she got a slap across the face. Chasm was not the kind of man to splutter, "Here! Now, really, Ofelia, I mean to say . . ." He liked to watch the women fight; he egged Ofelia on, urging her to deliver a good black eye. He wrote her a couple of sonnets: surprisingly lifeless, in stiff *siglo de oro* Spanish.

"Oh, schoolmaster stuff," Ofelia murmured.

"What kind of poetry do you admire, Cleo?"

After a scowl of deliberation, "Paler and paler grow my lips. And still you bid them bleed," she intoned.

"Did you write that?"

She was offended. "No, it is a real poem—it is not homemade."

"Next time I will give you the store-bought variety."

Out of the fathomless unknown that his past and present, their future together, were to her, Ofelia asked only one question, and that one was a tease. "Will you permit our children to be Roman Catholic?"

"They can be monkeys as far as I'm concerned," said the Professor.

He feigned disappointment when the boy turned out white. "I imagined it fat and black and smiling, like Uncle Porfirio. He looks more like Aunt Jemima to me," he complained. Aunt Jemima was his name for the skinny and sullen Lupita. And thereafter he called the child Jemima, and then just Jem, in mock of the child's pinched forbidding pallor.

Ofelia had wanted to christen the child Netzahualcoyotl. "You're the one who didn't know there was anyone in Mexico before the conquistadores. This new nationalism overwhelms

me. why don't you go strike with the poor grape pickers?"
Chasm demanded. "Anyway, I thought the orders were that
the children be Catholic, not cannibals." Jem was christened
Nicolas Januarius after an uncle instead.

"Falcon," Ofelia murmured to the child. "My little falcon,
who is so fierce he never closes his eyes or eats, but if he did
eat would rip out beating hearts."

North Carolina did not suit the falcon's mother. It was the
sticks. It was no better than Chiapas. It was worse. The Ne-
groes were *malin*, but not witty, as Indians could be. Imagine
the plight of a nineteen-year-old Spanish wild-child taking tea
with the southern faculty wives, sitting out complaints about
that queer old Mr. Philpotts, who wouldn't donate any of his
old furniture or clothes to the garage sale benefiting St. Mat-
thew's because he said he *liked* all his old junk. Well, some
people should be put in a *home* when they're too old and goofy
to know any better—he might do something really awful one
day.

Ofelia's days had been arranged for her by the community
before she arrived in Durham. Professor Chasm was already a
big favorite. Bridge clubs, committees, work with handi-
capped children. They were determined to make her feel at
home.

It was hard work to erect barriers between herself and the
committee ladies. Her English grew worse. She affected a
stilted accent and adopted quaint malapropisms at which she
herself could not restrain a smile.

"I am much much sorrow. I feel a *multitude* of regret, but
I am a Church of Rome," when assaulted for the church bazaar. "I am infinite sorry, but French the few language I am
able to speak," when invited to join the French Conversation
Club. Perhaps she could instruct their little gathering, be a
sort of presiding genius over their conversational sorties?

"I am so stupid—I do not understand." She turned away,

but when the suggestion was pursued, Ofelia said that she saw too much of teachers to presume to be one herself.

"My God, it's enough to drive one to drink," said Charles gleefully. Chasm drank and wrote. Ofelia drank and rode. She was too proud to seek consolation in her maid, so she found it as she had in Chiapas. An elderly admirer had placed a chestnut hunter at her disposal. But her husband curtailed the riding by saying, offhand, "Of course, if conquests are what amuse you—and why ever not?—you can do a sight better than that embezzling old fart who might land us all in jail one day."

There was still the flame between them, which not even the redneck royalty could quench. Chasm behaved badly, Ofelia behaved badly, but each with sufficient charm not to endanger his career. Professor Chasm conducted himself as he rode: pitching forward, back, and side to side but, like a stunt clown, never quite falling off. Only giving spectators a scare.

It was Jem who changed everything. He was her falcon, electrifying the dusty days which dawdled into nights, without sunsets, without twilights.

She no longer drank. The child disapproved; he turned his back to her when her kisses smelled of brandy. She wouldn't let her husband hold the boy. "Your hands shake too much." She teased Chasm until one day he picked up the child and threatened to drop him out the window if she didn't give over. Ofelia did not forgive him—he had called her a nag, too—but again they found each other ruinously attractive. As in the first year, until Jem was born, they never got out of bed. Charles almost got fired for canceling too many classes, but he had a couple of successful books out by now to ballast his career.

The child born of this embittered love thrived on it. Casimir slept and sang and ate all day.

"I don't like fat things," said Ofelia, clinging to Jem, now three years old, and watchful, disdainfully silent, because his lisp irritated him. Since threatening Jem's skull, Chasm was not allowed near the child, and ignored him in revenge. Anyone who hoped to make a hit with Mrs. Bocanegra Chasm petted the plain child, likely to bite, and not the baby. Lupita looked after Casimir.

"Dog, he only bites fat and ugly people," Ofelia said in delight. "Can you imagine? He hates them just as I do."

North Carolina was crammed with the fat and ugly, but when Professor Chasm's contract was up, he intended to sign on for another three years.

Why couldn't they go to England?

"Because I've just come from England."

Why couldn't they go *back* there?

"Because I've got a job here."

Why couldn't he find work in England?

"Because an assistant professor with an Oxford degree gets paid as much at an American university as the Regius Professor of History at Oxford, and there's more fun in spending it."

"Rich slave. Why couldn't we be poor in England?"

"Because you would find academic towns in England possibly more crammed full of fat-arsed refinement than Durham, North Carolina. At least here it is vastly entertaining fraudulence. There, it makes one cry."

A disturbing glare fastened upon the Professor for introducing her into this distasteful world.

And then the Restoration, the rake's return. Chasm had been offered a job at Georgetown.

They were making their way north, like birds after winter. No more dusty cornfields, no more mosquito-whine chats on porch gliders, no more Dairy Queen. They were moving to Washington, where those frank and brave ideals on which

America had been founded were made law, Chasm told her. And the shops will be open later: you can get around a bit. She envisaged it as a city-state, an Athens without plague, a Carthage before the salt. Chasm read her the *Federalist Papers* and the letters of men like Thomas Jefferson and John Adams, and she forgot altogether what she had learned of southern cities. When she got there she remembered she was bored by government and politics, she couldn't drive, her son didn't let her drink, and she went stir crazy.

It didn't help that Chasm and the boys took to the capital like mother's milk. She was alarmed and resentful that the children seemed to be having such fun—had forgotten who they were, as she put it. They played baseball and basketball in empty lots, set off firecrackers in the backyard, tried to feed their father exploding cigars and make him sit on whoopie cushions, and when he outsmarted them they screamed with laughter all the same. They learned to speak American. Later, when they were fourteen and twelve, they blared rock music and were never home unless locked in. When Jem was caught trying to hot-rod a diplomat's family car, Mrs. Chasm decided it was time the boys be taken to Mexico.

"I want my children to see their grandfather before he dies," she announced. "He has no other grandsons."

Bocanegra was still working hard. His manner was more raucous, more wheedling than Mrs. Chasm remembered; perhaps he was just glad to see them.

"I could see that the Professor was a gentleman and a scholar," he boasted. "Not *mierdas de gallina*, like Gaspar and Abelardo."

The boys were passed around that rotting circle of Spanish exiles and stroked, while Bocanegra pointed out their virtues.

That magnificent coloring! His own blue-black hair, his dead wife's olive skin, and eyes like the North Sea. Tall, too. But Nicolas could do with a little fattening up, hey?

Ifigenia and Consuelo were married to junior partners of Bocanegra's: men all promise and no future. Bocanegra was too frightened of being cheated or conspired against to entrust his daughters to anyone of consequence, but they hadn't yet caught on to the deal. Bocanegra gave his girls fur coats, fat allowances, and trips abroad, and kept them attentive with squeezes of the hand and hints as to what might lie in store for their husbands.

Bocanegra died with his boots on soon after the Chasms' visit, leaving behind him a closely worked and airtight will true to a man beneficent abroad and grudging at home. The business he left not to his sons-in-law but to a subordinate no one remembered having seen before, while the bulk of his money and property went over his daughters' heads altogether, and to his English grandsons, with Chasm as trustee until the boys turned twenty-one. ("Only seven years until we can leave the bastard strapped," said Jem.) Consuelo and Ifigenia and their families were left with only the flat in Mexico City and its uncomfortable armchairs to scrap over.

Jem, admiring his grandfather's instinct for creating with one neat turn a mess he would not be around to see cleaned up, also made himself a will. If he ever died, his belongings would go—not to the Jesuits; they were surely even more grasping than his brother—to Casimir. Anyway, Casimir would make such an attractive sole heir, good at making the gold diggers mop up his crocodile tears.

In the meantime Mrs. Chasm, who had money of her own by a similar arrangement of her unhappy mother's, abandoned any pretense of making Jem go to school. Casimir was left at junior high, and for the next three years Jem and his mother careered across the earth's surface. Wherever they stopped long enough, Jem found himself a tutor; he was prepared to learn anything, but from no one for more than a month. He left behind broken hearts in each station of the Foreign Legion: Cairo, Toledo, Berlin, Beirut.

From his mother, Jem learned how to deal with maîtres d'hôtel and to help ladies in stiletto heels across cobblestones with an authoritativeness that marked his solicitude from a kept boy's. From his mother, he learned of the degradation to which men bring women; he was treated to tirades against a husband who was knocking off all the pouting tarts in his class—"Someday he will be invited either to marry the Miss Mary Jo or Sue Ellen, or to leave his job"—and who had once threatened to chuck his son out the window because the boy's grandeur was already too menacing.

Jem vowed never to drink or to philander.

In the course of their travels the two surfaced occasionally in Washington. Jem could not keep his mother away a full year: she began tugging the lead back to Professor Chasm, to tease and jab at him. Jem could never understand it, after all the horrors she had recounted. When his parents were under the same roof he could neither eat nor sleep. One summer he petrified the household with stomach pains that made him scream. By a curious sympathy, Ofelia assumed some of Jem's ailments, too. They shared a sickroom. She didn't care about her own symptoms, but she took Jem to Switzerland to have a specialist diagnose his complaints. Jem was deemed highstrung, Ofelia had stomach cancer.

They were in Geneva when the diagnosis came. Ofelia shut herself up in her hotel bedroom. At nightfall Jem knocked on the door and brought her the newspapers and a bar of chocolate. He curled up beside her in the featherbed and read her the headlines of the *Herald Tribune,* while she made a champagne glass out of the silver paper of the chocolate wrapper and tried to make her new lap dog drink brandy from it.

"Well, Falcon," she said, when he had finished reading, "the doctor thinks that you are faking." She gave him a hard stare, and he glared back, mortified. "He thinks I should put you in a strict boarding school and that we should have no more nonsense about stomachaches and whatnot. What do you think about that?"

"I think if you put me in a strict boarding school you would never sleep an entire night through, knowing that I would be back to slit your throat for it."

Ofelia read him the rest of the doctor's report. Jem said nothing but began pulling the puppy's ears, hard, until the dog bit him and Jem threw it across the room. His mother slapped him, almost absentmindedly, and Jem walked out.

For the next year they traveled faster, while the cancer spread. Ofelia finally grew so jealous of even the crushes he had on his tutors that his education was abandoned. "He seems to learn better without a teacher. He is too proud to be taught."

Jem would explore the town in which they found themselves during the morning while Ofelia arranged her long black coils of hair, which, as she wasted away, seemed increasingly like a fibrous black python consuming her. Jem looked at the cathedral, mosque, or temple, the marketplace, the ruin, or the palace. He smoked and drank mint tea, played chess with the café elders, gambled at a street corner. He hung around the docks, talking to the sailors, the stevedores, the merchants. He read voraciously. He wrote voluminous diaries and poems.

At around two Ofelia would summon Jem along with pots of coffee and a pile of magazines and tobacco, and demand a vivid and precise account of the site in which they were stationed.

They would lie across her bed all afternoon, smoking,

reading Spanish, German, Arab fashion magazines and cutting out paper dolls.

Before, his pride had been in designing clothes for his mother's dressmaker to make up for her, in picking out her jewels and dresses and coats and handbags for the evenings. Now she weighed no more than a paper doll, and could no longer wear her clothes or summon up the interest to have new ones made. She wrapped herself up in a dressing gown all day, and wore one of her dozen black box-shaped dresses when they went to dinner or the cinema every evening.

And now her paper minions vied with one another's magnificence, decked out in costumes more elaborate than those of ladies at the court of Eugénie or Catherine when they were commanded to appear in men's clothing; that assembly of bedizened pageboys and powdered Don Juans must have been akin to the intricacies of Jem's court.

He concocted stages, too, from tissue boxes, on which his favorites performed plays that he had written while others for that evening were in disgrace. The mornings of scouring mosques and rococo palaces were fired into the gold tissue and pearl hatpin-minareted jewel boxes in which his creatures performed. He made a replica of the Teatro del Luz in San Ildefonso de Nepomuceno: a turn of the century Roman revival in pink and green marble.

It had been Mrs. Chasm's idea that Jem should be an artist. She feared that he had a scholarly turn of mind—worse, a love of pedantry: he had irritated her many times by correcting her pronunciation, pointing out misusages, and she was frightened that he would turn out another academic. She tried to shame him out of his superciliousness, his taste for dry subjects. Ofelia stressed what a dingy, middle-class profession teaching was and prodded him into higher flights of fancy. She encouraged his inclination to pick things up and drop them, demanding fresh novelties of him at such a rate that Jem was obliged to skim. After all, she insisted, he would never have to make his living. He could pursue his tastes, exercise his fantasy. His commanding eye, his rare imagination.

Jem possessed the air of having grown up in the hotel bedrooms of a lady. He was uncompromisingly à la carte—the tyrannical son whose sunken pallor testifies to his mother's not daring to forbid him to have only baked Alaska for supper—whereas Casimir was menu fixe. When he met them sometimes for the summer in Europe, Ofelia impelled Casimir to maneuver his fictitious appetite through seven courses or, worse still, would say, pinstripe black eyebrow lifted, "I daresay Casimir would prefer hamburger and ice cream; however, I cannot quite face asking. Falcon, would you ask if they can make such a thing." (After she died, Jem, in retrospective rebellion, for a long time ate nothing but cheeseburgers and milkshakes.) Or she would question Casimir, with a feigned interest more damning still, on the fate of the Redskins, and when he expounded would say, much too quickly and eyes wandering, "I see. I see."

Sometimes she talked to Jem about getting some property in Canada, a wooden house on a river in the woods, a fishing camp. He stared.

Ofelia died on a scorching day in Cuernavaca.

They sent the body down to Chiapas. Chasm rode out to the canyons behind the Bocanegra estate, beyond the scrubby plots of squatters' barnyards to the black pine ravines, to scatter her ashes. Carmens go up in flames. Lupita was the only one who cried.

She never went to England. That she haunts the Indian villages and evergreen forests still seems sadly in order.

. . .

I guess it all comes down to money, because now that Jem and Casimir at the ages of seventeen and fifteen were rich men, they didn't have to pay heed to anybody. Jem didn't have to be a paid companion, and Casimir didn't have to be a dumb quarterback. They stayed in Mexico City for almost six months while the estate was settled. For a woman who knew she was going to die, Mrs. Chasm had been remarkably free and easy about her will. Jem and Casimir decorously divided the spoils, with a few tidbits thrown to Chasm.

Jem confiscated the jewelry and the wardrobes of clothing that nobody bothered to pretend the Mexican nieces could squeeze into. "They are mine," he said fiercely. "I designed them."

"I'm not going to scrap over them with you. You can wear a different ball gown and tiara to dinner every night as far as I'm concerned," said the Professor.

And Jem went into mourning: a black suit a little too short at the wrist and ankle, a diamond and emerald bracelet or a pearl earring in his lapel like a legionnaire's ribbon. He let Casimir have most of the art they had collected in their travels, and threw to his father a few starchy impressionists of Bocanegra's. Jem hooked for himself one small picture, a panel from the Works of Saint Nicholas: the crimson and charcoal-gray saint on tiptoes, tossing the moneybags through a lavender window, while inside the three dowerless girls and their guardian—crimped platinum blondes and a pimp if you ever saw one—were tucked up in bed, merry as grigs.

"We might get you a house to accommodate all your loot," suggested the Professor, after Jem had been idling around Washington in between schools. "Now that you are such a rich man, it might be in order."

"Not in this sanctimonious sewer of a country."

"Suit yourself, little orphan boy, you've got the cash."

Casimir was hugging the Professor tightly. "What will happen to you, Papa Doc, if we leave you?"

"Oh, I suppose I'll have to shine shoes."

Chasm had other possibilities in mind. He had been offered a fellowship at All Souls and was tempted. He was out of luck in Washington, what with the Democrats coming into office: democracy with a soft underbelly and a hominy grits whine. The pay at All Souls was piddling (carfare) but the obligations nil, and in middle age he had conceded to a comical respect for English institutions. He had started dreaming of starched scouts and two solid meals at high table and an even solider cellar below. It would be a fine thing too, after the flaming pinks of American academia, to find himself the least cantankerously reactionary man at the table.

Altogether, Jem and Casimir might be well advised to buy a house in England, and he pressed the case ingeniously. He, of course, would rarely be there, his commitments in America and Western Europe being such a damned relentless nuisance, but if his sons intended to learn how to read and write, they had little alternative but to find a decent tutorial establishment in Oxford. Jem balked. He wanted to go live in Mexico, he insisted. He was going to take over the estancia in Chiapas, which his grandfather had left him. (Chasm had put it on the market after Bocanegra's death, but no one would touch it.) Professor Chasm was exasperated as always by the child's puling arrogance—so full of himself, and yet such a sissy. Seventeen-year-old boys don't go run large estates in the Mexican highlands, he pointed out. And what an estate.

"It was a bedsore on your grandfather's bum, that house," said Chasm. "He wished he'd never got it. Always something wrong. If the roof hadn't fallen in, then Jorgito had just strangled Guadelupe." And who knows what had happened to it by now? No one had lived there year round in ages.

"Houses must be lived in, Jemmy. Sell that house or let it

tumble. It's beyond repair. If you pour more money into it, the country's bound to go Commie and the rat trap will be confiscated by the Chiapan National Liberation Front. Sell while you can."

If it hadn't been clear from the start that Jem had no desire in the least to go live in Mexico by himself, his father by this tack might have talked him into it eventually, but as it was they struck a compromise. The estate wasn't sold but put on ice, and Jem instead went to England with his family.

Lupita came to keep house in Belbroughton Road, and Casimir and Jem were enrolled at an expensive crammer's in town. No more Loti-loving Turks tutoring Jem in Islam. No more cheerleaders for Casimir. They soon became instead as English as they were to become, and minor legends about town.

Casimir was not merely a survivor but a lax despot. His imaginative vigor lay in his ability to make chameleon trans-formations, to hunt down prevailing fantasies and embody them. Tramp, gigolo, desert traveler, jazz musician: every man's woman and every woman's man. In high school in America he had been a jock known for his ability to make girls "go all the way" with him. In England, where sex, as he put it, was profoundly beside the point, he was famous for having the biggest overdraft in his class. He endeared everyone to him with his raucous and insinuating high spirits; he was the kind of teenage hero that died in the war.

Jem was something else again. His refusal to compromise, to change his clocks when he crossed time zones, made him a somewhat spectral figure. When he teetered down the hall in his barbarian mourning, his thinness stiffly splayed, knees glued together, he looked like an absurd dignitary such as one used to see in hotel dining rooms in Montreux or Lausanne: a deposed claimant to one of the Balkan kingdoms.

He was as rude and grasping in his appetite for learning as

he was effete in his other ways, and no one was surprised that after eight months of his first bout with regular schooling Jem should have won a scholarship to read English at Balliol. That he should eventually leave without a degree seemed equally fitting.

Five

Was it right to leave my mother all alone, my father wanted to know, surprised and none too pleased that I was planning to come to England that summer. After all, his work brought him to New York so often, perhaps I had best stay with Mummy, and he would take me away for a couple of weeks in August to Haiti again, or to Barbados. But Mummy, who indulged me in everything, was anxious for me to go, and so she was left in that dark intoxicating grave of a house with Eustacius for company. I imagined them sitting downstairs in the kitchen, knocking back the bourbon and telling stories of my great-grandmother, the indomitable beauty built like an ocean liner, who never went more than a yard from the house, and then under a sunshade with maid and Pekingese for company, but who knew every hand towel in the linen room and had made every one of her eight children go to college. I can hear now the sound of their cackling laughter rising from the kitchen like the ghosts of black slaves singing in their chains; I mustn't think about it lest it drag me under. I loved it too much, that house, and confronting the workaday world was like being dredged up from the river, away from the strong sweet undercurrents.

Jem was sitting on the railing outside Customs in a sea of
chauffeurs and paid welcomers proffering handwritten signs
for tours and missions. I saw him through the smoked glass
doors as they swung open and shut: he didn't see me. He really
had become a knock-kneed Frankenstein. He was huddled behind a newspaper behind a cigar, behind dark glasses. He was
all closed off. He spotted me as I came through the doors and,
without seeming to look up, jumped off the railing, throwing
cigar and paper on the floor, and with two harsh kisses swung
me up in the air. I had forgotten these instant transformations
each Chasm was capable of effecting: from the moribund to
manic animation.

"Where are your bags, Scarlet? You don't look as if you
travel light anymore."

"A man's got them. How did you know it was me?"

Jem pretended to consider. "I knew you'd be the one who
wasn't toiling and sweating over a trolley. Americans are too
sturdy and moral to get porters, the English too mean."

"And what am I if not American or English?"

"You're neither, like me. We're changelings. Now wait
here." Jem jumped the queue and came back to bundle me
and my suitcase into a cab. The black, sweet, clammy night
air of London was like a fallen cake. Jem pushed down the
window as far as it would go and the wind barely stirred his
hair. I couldn't soak it in deeply enough. Every exhilarated
arrival in a strange city by night seemed only a forecast of this
one: Jem by my side hurtling past avenues of swan-necked
platinum lampposts exuding yellow fog-light, along an empty
highway. I was too excited to talk: the words glittered and
broke in my head before they reached the surface, so Jem
tossed out conversation at random, mimicking Casimir's man-
nered delivery. What news, Scarlet, what news? Professor

Chasm out of circulation and Stephanie gone back to her aged parents for a spell. Casimir in quarantine—just back from Southeast Asia *black* with diseases he had picked up playing guerrilla at the Thai border.

"So we've got the house to ourselves, Scarlet, you might as well settle in for a long winter's stay. Don't fret about your pa—Desmond hadn't a clue when you're due to arrive; as a matter of fact, I did a little disinformation work and called to tell him I'd discovered you were flying Sunday. You're vague about itineraries yourself, Scarlet; I finally called New York to find out if you'd left yet and what flight you were on. I got an elderly gentleman who sounded as if he'd missed the last ride on the Underground Railway. I asked where you were. 'She over there.' Where? The other side, he tells me. So you're still among the living, Scarlet. I had my doubts, and Rastus didn't ease them any.

"Are you hungry, tired, Jezebel? Do you feel like a cool bath and bed? Can I take you home with me and never let you go?"

Jem doubled up, his voice coming muffled from between his knees sneaking sidelong glances at me until I slid over and took him in my arms, kissed him on the nose and chin, and he laughed. I drank it again, the rich stuff of his hair standing out stiffly around the small skull, the eyes that made one always aware of the entire globe, wet jewels tumbling out of their sockets, eyes the color of an oil spill, petrol-green, the skin too with an unnatural tint to it, an olive that was metallic.

"What did you say to me?"

"I said, can I never let you go?"

It was as if two years had been only a breath between the stretches of a secret pact, a long love affair, and I had to make myself remember that I didn't know Jem, that he wasn't mine, that we weren't even friends.

But it was he, and not Casimir or Daddy, who found out

when I was arriving and who rode down from Oxford to meet my plane, despite his horror of airports, and he who was carrying me away with him, east of the sun, west of the moon, like the husband whose face the girl never sees until she holds a candle over him one night, wakes him with a drop of wax, and is sent home to her woodcutter parents. What was the lesson? Don't try to know too much. Love and be silent.

It was no time before Jem and I started to wrangle, worrying niceties to shreds. That was what happened when you lived too much alone, when idleness and discontent joined forces to create a life in fantasy: you dreamed up people to whom you could talk with perfect freedom and you held long, rapturous, yet curiously samey conversations with them in your head. The situations became imaginary and complex; you rescued them from peril nightly. All this I did for Jem and Jem for me, so I understood it, but still there was nothing I could do when each of us was so anxious for the answers to his heart's question and the other was out of tune. I felt remorseful but frozen into an attitude of indifference, and I didn't like that idiot look he had, showing the whites of his eyes like a horse.

The M4 had disengaged itself from suburbs, from lightless beauty parlors and bingo halls, and now the black cab was jolting through darkness. From the ring road to North Oxford you could see no spires or domes, not even the oxidized green globe of the Observatory. In the dark it could be a suburb of Berlin, and Jem, sighing and wriggling on the seat beside me, an unknown passenger. I reached over and stroked the spikes of hair from his eyes, just to see him flinch, and almost expected the shock of having assailed a stranger on the street, that Jem might recoil, suggesting I had mistaken him for someone else. The cab drew up at the door of the house, and

Jem, cursing and muttering over the swindle of the cab fare—
seventy pounds—dragged my suitcase up three flights of stairs,
and burst open the door to the drawing room.

The room was unchanged. During his year in Spain the
upstairs had fallen into the ways of a rotting garçonnière, he
explained, with Casimir roller-skating across the parquet, for-
getting gnawed chicken legs in every armchair. But Jem, for a
hotel-suite child, possessed a thorough bourgeois keenness for
housekeeping. On his return, he had dispatched Lupita,
whitewashed the walls, and aired the room of its foxhole dank-
ness; he scrubbed, he scoured, he reinstated his memorials—
"the ones I wasn't able to palm off on you." The same mammoth Buddha, the same rickshaw unloading dead goodies
onto the black and white floor, a feast of fanged and snarling
lilies that gave off the scent of diseased flesh. But the center-
piece of the arrangement was a box of Chinese takeout and a
tin trunk brimming over with filthy white silk jackets, tied in
knots, and two-toned shoes.

Casimir was laid out on the green satin sofa when we came
in. Jem barely glanced at him. He started kicking the trunk
down the hall to Casimir's door, muttering, "Slattern. Lewd
pig. I told you to get this trash out of the hall by *six*."

Casimir did not look black, but very white indeed—so wan
that Jem was chastened into making up his bed for him.

"Now, stay *put*. I don't want to see you come drooping
down the hall again looking pathetic and unwashed," Jem
called after him, as Casimir drifted back to bed.

Even in sickness I could see that he had turned out an ugly
beauty: the broken nose, the long black curls, the big, lasci-
vious red mouth gave him a satyr's face in jangling colors. He
had shot up in the last year or so and now was even taller than
Jem or his father, but broad-shouldered, barrel-chested, taper-
ing down to slim hips, almost dainty wrists. He dressed like a

five-and-dime toreador, but his charm was as if he didn't know he possessed it.

Jem differed. "Jesus!" he exploded. "You make the boy sound like a man's after-shave. Yes, Casimir has all the allure of someone who can get up at dawn in Oxford and walk to London to see his dying grandmother, arrive at the Chelsea Hospital in time to charm her back to life, and then sulk if he can't persuade everyone to go on to a Lebanese discotheque afterwards."

I shrugged. Casimir was flawless. As far as I was concerned, he could do no wrong.

Jem started. "That's simply not true," he said coldly. "Casimir is very treacherous. He lies through his teeth. Stay away from him. I'll drop you like a hot potato if you get lice and syphilis and whatever else the boy is riddled with."

Jealousy: the initial, the final, the implicating motive. What it spins out in art, it lops off our guts. Casimir, the unjealous, once said, "Jem can do *anything* better than I can. But he's so frightened he won't be able to that he does nothing instead. He even festers beautifully."

All I knew was that Casimir was gay and easy company who made a trip to the grocery store a revel and a quest. When I was with Jem I became peeled to a new moon of myself—a new moon that tried to speak the King's English for a change.

Jem's plans had been rudely jostled. He had counted on Casimir's already being swept into a back room before I arrived, and it took all his presence of mind not to sulk at the disorder. All we needed now was for Professor Chasm to lope in the door, sideways, his eyes rolling behind the windowpane spectacles like a rabid dog's, as Jem remarked. Been to Spain for a little research? He hadn't been to the corner.

Professor Chasm had taken up with a quarrelsome blonde married to a colleague of his, and Jem followed their goings-on closely. He knew what they were up to every night of the week. He knew when his father sneaked her off to dinner in Thame and even there they couldn't be quite incognito, because she had to be sick on the floor, or goose the waiter, or anything to keep Chasm interested: "It's worse than taking the first Mrs. Rochester to dinner in a market town on an off night."

And now this creature had taken to turning up at All Souls and harassing the porters.

"What a thing to happen to a self-deluding liar, to have his compartments shuffled. But what a pair: aging roué and raddled vamp, trapped in a deathlock of lust—in the Europa Motel."

It made me uneasy, this spying. "Why bother to find out?"

"When I was a child, I wanted to be a saint. The only thing I've wanted to be since is a spy. Perhaps I wouldn't be such an ace at it, either—you watch people begin to fuck up and want to go in and rearrange."

"And Stephanie?"

"She lost a baby. Does nothing. A little silent weeping. A good soldier. I'd tell her to get out now before they do manage to have a child, but she wouldn't take it well from me."

It was only sitting in this field of black and white, like a heraldic device, that I noticed how Jem had changed. He had filled out a little, looked almost well fed. That Polish goose had been stuffing him. He looked more complacent, too. And he came in colors. Black suit, black sneakers, but his shirt was of a silk the color of raspberry ice. Jem was affronted when I took the shimmering stuff between my fingers, marveled at the shade of it. Not his doing, he protested. Casimir had brought it back from Bangkok, this shirt with arms cut for a gorilla, an American. "What are you mauling me for? Get your hands off, for Christ's sake!"

"But you always wore black before—all this color, it's blinding."

"I didn't always wear black, what nonsense. Jesus, I'm not Greta Garbo, I'm a growing boy. There's no always about it. Anyway, you only knew me for about three weeks. Who are you to make such pronouncements?"

"I liked it."

"Well, you're sick."

Jem was plying me with liquor now. He had brought out a bottle of hundred-proof vodka and a bottle of Armenian champagne. We swigged from tall glasses. Jem was looking at me out of the corner of his eye again—at my wrists and ankles, measuring them, spanning them surreptitiously.

"When did you get so pretty, Jezebel? Last time I thought I was the only man on earth who could see what a piece of heaven was in your throat and back, but by now you must be knee deep in broken hearts. Do they let you run around, your mother and that Negro slave? They ought to keep you under house arrest. You ought to be reading books at your age and not meeting people."

No broken hearts, I told him, only a few disturbances. He teased me into spilling the beans and I told him about the Spanish teacher and some hoods I had met in Central Park, swallowing and prolonging with a stutter the words of this poor narration. Jem seemed irritated that, if there had to have been other flames in my life, they should prove such piddling ones.

"Your father is quite right," Jem said. "You should have kept the book and got the Spanish teacher sacked."

"But he left anyway."

"Well, as blackmail, then."

"What would I have blackmailed him *for*—ten free Spanish lessons? He's a pauper, the poor thing. Why else would he be teaching at a girls' school?"

Jem cleared his throat. "Do I really need to explain?"

"Oh, he wasn't a lecher at all, just a fool."

"But you should have got him sacked without a reference.

Let *him* become a croupier in the Pyrenees. Well, at least you get rid of your boyfriends quickly. But I don't like it, Jezebel, it doesn't ring true," he complained. "There's something flat and lukewarm about these little excursions into perversity—you don't take them very far, do you?

"This is what puzzles me: Why do I see no spark? I peer into your round blue eyes like an aquarium, so clear, not eyes at all. One expects to see little fish, octopuses, squids paddling about in them. I feel like plunging my fingers into them, taking a swim. You say nothing and when you do open your mouth you say things which shock me by their callousness, things you've seen which should shock you and don't. It makes me want to hit you, just to knock some feeling into you. It's not glamorous not to be shocked, it's autistic. You shouldn't just be on, like a television set. Perhaps you're frightened of seeming judgmental, along with everyone else these days. Well, it's a piece of dangerous lunacy, this new prohibition against morality. You've got to fight for the free world, Jezebel, stand up for Jesus.

"Have you ever read any poetry, Jezebel? Oh, I know you've read the hot-handed wonderboys, but wait till you get to the eighteenth century. Take a lesson from that shivering insect Pope, who burst a blood vessel at every glimpse of corruption and fraud, and knew it was his duty to pin it down and lash it. He didn't ask was it any of his business, like someone watching a street accident.

> *Ask You what provocation I have had?*
> *The strong antipathy of good to bad.*
> *When Truth or Virtue an Affront endures*
> *Th'Affront is Mine, my friend, and should be Yours.*

"You can't be God's alone, Jezebel. You're mine, and your country's, and your family's and everyone else's. I tell you nothing but the most faded commonplaces, but you seem never to have heard them before," he concluded accusingly.

He had reassumed his housekeeper bossiness. He stuck me in a bath, he made up my bed on the chaise longue and found I had outgrown it, so he put me in Lupita's old room. But when I emerged, steamed and scented, I wouldn't be put to bed. I wanted true confession from Jem, or at least to discomfit him in turn. He was too nannylike in stripping one of privacy while standing upon his own. Where did this spoiled idler come off as a fighter for the free world, a defender of the family. What was his war effort, I wanted to know; what had brought about this conversion. But Jem would not be drawn, he was pinched with exhaustion. The curtain had come down, but I was still in my red velvet seat, waiting for more.

"What about Oxford; what does one do here all day?"

"The hellhole," he muttered angrily.

"Do you go to the Bodleian?"

"No, it is infested with scabrous teen anarchists."

What was he going to do with himself, then? What was going to become of him?

"I am having suits made me," he said at last. "Three in black silk, paper thin, that Casimir brought back from the East, one in black wool with a red pin stripe. I am going to stop being an orphan, and become a man of leisure. In a few months' time I will be twenty-one, and if one is going to do nothing it is time to stop floundering and lolling about whitening one's nose against shop windows, and start doing nothing decisively. I am going to go live in Mexico, in this house that has been knocking on my heart's door for years now while I clowned and agonized and delayed. You see, I wanted to be a great man," Jem explained, "a hero for all time. But now it is enough only to live."

"You're not going to write?"

He winced, despite himself. "No talking about writing.

You can do whatever you like in the wilderness. Nobody is there to check up on you." Jem was slipping away again, skipping town just as I'd caught him again. I'd killed so much time just till I could smell the sweetness of his breath, sink in the blue of his eyes' whites, and he was already lost to me. When?

"When all my suits fit. I keep sending them back because the bottoms bag or the shoulders are padded as a drag queen's falsies. Don't look so disapproving; you will feel it, too, this panic despair of not being able to find an existing occupation you could conceivably be suited to."

I was unconvinced.

"I have been trying to give guilt the slip," Jem said, more truthfully.

"You? I always thought you were ruthless, Jem."

"Only about other people. I saw, suddenly, that the fallings-short with which I've battered my conscience can either be corrected or ignored. Like waiters. If you complain about the eggs, either you get a new batch or they pretend not to hear. No self-laceration."

A tall order for a figure whose every sunken hollow and jutting bone expressed a self-scrutiny stirred to suffering, a passion such as one saw, sometimes, in seventeenth-century Spanish crucifixions. So much for covering the scars in raspberry silk, so much for the debutante rounds. Let him dance.

When I arrived filthy from Paddington the next afternoon my father's flat was a bower of powder-gray bliss as always. Ensconced in a cane-backed chair was a preserved white monkey of a lady at whom my father was gazing over the rim of his teacup, as raptly as if she were telling him his fortune in the leaves.

"My love, have you met Mrs. Palafox?"

"But naturally," she answered for me. "We met when little miss was ten years old and she came to see the new aviary."

Oh-oh-oh. Scarlet lacquered fingernails scraped up the skin of my cheek to say, with a feverish hum, "Bit of all right, wouldncha say?"

It was hard to know what to say.

"We're kind of kissing cousins, doncha know?"

Oh yes, there was a strand of strung-out sodden southern blood between us, a Louisiana Congo trail of blood, of glory-be; two cousins in the 1890s who liked to pole down the Bayou to Leopoldville and shoot possum together, which meant that I could call her Cousin Clothilde if I liked.

"But my papa was such a rebel we never set foot south of the Mason-Dixon line: he thought it depleted the blood—and grits always stuck in my throat. But you're a true-blue *créole*, Desmond tells me. Now tell me, babypie, can you talk it and everything?"

"*Un petty po.*" I could talk about as much Creole as Mary Magdalene, and what I could, as my father well knew, came from the summer in Haiti and not the old plantation.

But squawk, squawk. People were easy to please. "Now that's what I call glamor. I mean to say, that's rich, black, mercurial *magic*, if you like, eh?"

She had witnessed the coming together of particles, Ofelia Chasm, Jem and Casimir, me—this macaw. That was magic, if you liked. I endured the pincers once again, but when Daddy told me afterwards, "You made a remarkable hit with Mrs. Palafox," I only said, "She made a remarkable pinch with me."

And when I next saw Jem I had to tell him, "There was a flaming old lady there when I stepped in the door, and she's left me black and blue."

"Who is that?" Jem had perked up at this confirmation of

my father's depravity, but when I described Mrs. Palafox he was disappointed.

"Oh, her."

"Do you know Mrs. Palafox—I mean since the bird-house?"

"Not well, but often. She's a pal of my father's too. He says she's the only ugly woman he can bear talking to."

She was the kind of American that is almost extinct today. Dragged across Europe as a little girl, until she trilled a mélange of opera Italian, couturier French, and bullfight Spanish, with an overlay of Etonian slang. And enchanted Europeans with her Americanisms. A sort of southern charm, New England asperity, Wild West. That wonderful Yankee outspokenness: an outspokenness that was pure manner, a miracle of facade.

"Outspokenness is not just putting your big foot in it, but sloshing it around," she had said.

She had a jaguar prowl that suggested independence, but there was always someone to carry the bags. She had been passionately in love with her husband, who was a vapid womanizer and a big-game hunter, and much of their marriage was spent in the bushveldt. After his death thirty years ago, she had become one of the directors of the New York Zoological Gardens. "The Chamulas believed that everyone's animal spirit lived high in the Chiapas mountains in a corral, and if your animal escaped, which they were always trying to do, you would be ill or mad, until you got it back in its corral. It is fitting that such a bestiary on wheels should spend her time keeping the animals in cages. I wonder does she ever feel on the wrong side of the bars?" Jem mused.

I could not share his rancor. It was a rich old lady job, and I could tell she did not really like being a charity hag. She was a little scornful of admirers who wanted to make her mythical;

their proprietary adulation left her cold. She missed sleeping under the stars with a rifle and a man.

But the old, even the rich old, have got to make do—with their trained nurses and their flunkies and what friends left who will have them.

Six

~~~~~~

What was what he was like these days, the man of leisure?
Some lunacy bred of idleness led him through dark, winding
passages of speculation and when you said something in reply,
his eyes wandered with such desperate resentment you were
shamed into silence. For the first time, his painfully keen appetite for knowledge was turning colicky. He no longer had
the violence and hope to seize novelty by the scruff of the neck
and worry at it, as he used to. He didn't listen any more. He
had got a fright in Salamanca, but all he could say of his year
there was that there was an agate and chiseled silver Sacrifice
of Abraham in the college chapel, that in winter the sky was
reddened by flamingos flying to North Africa, and that the
Jesuits were Marxists. When he returned to Oxford, he made
no attempt to mend fences, but stayed away from the university in a similar show of disillusion and mistrust. He had found
the citadel of learning to be envious, bored, faction-ridden,
that scholars could be as silly as other people. Except for the
one or two maniacally odd and desiccated dons with whom
Jem kept up friendships, teased and insulted into a moment's
faltering, girlish animation, he had estranged himself from
that spiked quadrangle of gargoyles watching one another that

was the university. He had encouraged benefactors and misled them, he had made enemies. In Oxford, that left one with nothing but department stores and skinheads.

Jem skulked in the threadbare Biedermeier coziness of North Oxford. And when people in New York or London asked me about the colleges, I gaped. I didn't know there were any colleges in Oxford, only vegetable stores and the barber-shop.

As a recluse, Jem was able to imagine high life for himself: worlds of court costume, pearl-studded and stiff with gold, of conversation that was flight (miracles of nuance, self-reflecting surfaces), and of waltzes that were conversation. But when he had ventured to London balls, a perpetual cold daylight seemed to turn the maquillage to greasepaint caked on mottled pug faces.

When he withdrew once again, it was with a new hardness without sparkle, a dulled greed. He continued to see people. He had a new dread of being stranded, accompanied by an emergent pack of necessities. Suddenly a shiny car seemed vital to take him to the tobacconist, a credit card for the Chinese takeout. He was frightened to appear in the street with a retinue smaller than a president's wife's. The flighty young ladies were dismissed, but he had replaced them with an entourage of undergraduates, bland and well heeled, but each with the morale of a Lion's Club lounge in Trieste: spiritually down and out.

He complained that I looked down on his friends, but if I felt mischievous I would say, "That divine Patrick—just what a man should be . . ." to see Jem choke and gorgonize me. When Magnus acted as if he might be taken with me, when he mentioned my name too persistently and began to rival Jem in the delivering of flowers and hacked verse, Magnus was dropped down the oubliette. If any of the boys showed signs of liking one another, Jem feared mutiny. Combined, they might develop their own interests and inclinations, might decide to drive to Sussex at midnight and catch the early morning ferry to France instead of setting off for the late-night show of *Macao* at the Electric; worse still, might go without him.

But the danger was not in their taking off, but in their staying. Although Jem thrived on being taken for drives, he found it difficult to dismiss the drivers when he was done. Once inside the house, these young men seemed to attach themselves by tentacles to the kitchen floor and stay. Passing the time of day, I believe the occupation is called. Exchanging pleasantries. There is a Boer custom known as up-sitting, Jem told me. (Those people had charm.) A man who wanted to marry a girl had to sit up with her all night long. Can you imagine the tedium of two fat red turkey cocks who had probably never laid eyes on each other before but possessed compatible herds of cattle, spinning out conversational magic in the hopje parlor throughout a long African night?

When Jem was driven to a frenzy by their staying, but felt too sorry for himself to kick them out, he would lock himself into his empty bedroom with an atlas, storming out at intervals to see if they had left yet. I suspected this need for admirers was to compensate for Casimir's defection: Casimir had a girl friend, a tiny waitress with spiky black hair and a white skin who said nothing but held Casimir's hand with great fervor. She was five or six years older than he, and Casimir spent most of his time in her furnished room across the river. Occasionally he came home to eat. Jem used to reproach me for not having secured Casimir's affections. "You could have had him, but you drove him away."

It could only be Jem who was leaning on the doorbell, milking the buzzer of its last gasp. I skidded outside in my slippers to its faltering, splenetic whine. Livid. I had said I wouldn't come to Oxford that night, sick of the flunkies. And there was Jem on the doorstep, still jamming the bell when I appeared, flanked by the three boys who had driven him to London. Jem's stilted smile looked foolish, desirous of approval. "The bell didn't seem to work very well."

"But you straightened it out," I said coldly. Slammed a whiskey bottle, an ice bucket, soda syphon before them in the sitting room, exchanged a few sentences with the boys, and went back to my room. Cursed the clones languorously while turning the pages of a book. At last I could hear Jem ushering them out, brisk as closing time. He burst into my room—he was never much of a knocker, but enjoyed SAS raids, eyes veering to see what abominations he had interrupted. Tonight, he slumped on the end of my bed with extinguished lights for a stare. It was the closest I had come to despising him. I got up and began emptying the ashtrays in the sitting room, clattering away stale drinks.

He followed, "Why couldn't you have rustled up your superior charms for a change?" he challenged. "Or at least kicked them out yourself? You have no trouble clearing a room when you choose."

"They are your curs."

"Oh, they call me master, but they hate me so." He grabbed the dustpan from my hand, muttering, "Zombie," and raked the room clean.

"Why are they always, always so damningly along for the ride?" he grumbled. "And if one's going nowhere, they just sit there expectantly, waiting for nothing to happen."

"I thought Patrick and Andrew drove *you*."

"I make them, I kick and scream until they've *got* to take me to Northumberland at dawn. If I didn't, their cars would rot in Holywell Street, accumulating parking tickets. I loathe people not exploiting their resources. I loathe people who wait to be shaken up like a handful of Mexican jumping beans."

"Why don't you get rid of them?"

"They are *my* resources," said Jem. "But I won't be turned on every night like the television set." He glared at me pointedly until I reminded him, "*You* came to see *me*."

"I was returning your calls. I thought I'd like to see *you* be the hostess. And a charming one you were, too—accomplished. Plenty of liquor, enough ice: that's the secret to a good party."

I went back to my room and again Jem followed. We sat side by side on the bed, looking straight ahead like passengers on a bus.

"Get rid of those boys, Jem."

"Listen here, Miss Babylon. You're the greediest and most exploitative of all. Good-time Charley. When things get dull, you go to your room."

"I hate to see you doing your tricks and not getting sawdust back."

Jem leaned back, chin on chest. "What wouldn't I do to have Casimir back again. For his sweet babble I would be down on my knees three days like Henry at Canossa." And then, in a change of tune, "We had better blow away this waitress friend of his. We'll hire a hit man and send her to junkie heaven."

But it wasn't the girl who was keeping Casimir across the river. He had had enough of Jem's crankiness for a while.

"Learn a little sweet talk," I told him. "You can be as sour as you like if you want to live by yourself, but if it's company you're after, there are concessions to be made."

"For instance?" Jem looked at his fingernails, superior and disbelieving. There was nothing so disagreeable as other people's lectures.

"Well, listening to what other people say does wonders, for a start. You needn't even laugh at their jokes, if you can look sincere enough. Call people by their names every now and then—everyone gets a secret thrill from hearing his name aloud. And don't talk about yourself so much. If you're going to take yourself so damned seriously, you can't afford to seem cynical about others." I tried to teach him how to look sincere, but we both started giggling and his mouth was too crooked: he looked as if he were going to be sick. And when I started to look sincerely at Jem, he cried, "Stop it! Don't you dare try it on me. Your frightful cowlike contentment is just what doesn't interest me."

I knew what he meant: I was familiar with this rage to hurt that other people's complacency could inspire, but it was hard keeping people in your pocket if you were too eager to snub them, too. They went away.

My parents had a smugness that decked itself out as self-deprecation. Mummy loved to sigh, "Well, I've always been sooo extravagant, and Daddy used to get so sore (I guess that's why he left) when I gave away everything I had to artists and little children—oh, to the point of *folie*, I guess. But life is short, we might as well be *très, très gaies*." When really what she meant was that she was generous and otherworldly, and Daddy was a petty tyrant. And Daddy in turn liked to carry on about his own unworldliness: how even when he hadn't had a bean he'd always known what was style—my eyes dropped to his green velvet jeans. "In '68, I told the Douglasses to snatch an Alma Tadema that was up at auction, but they turned up their noses: candybox art, and everyone was keen on blank canvases. Well now, my dear, Sotheby's has sold a *Roman Baths* for a hundred and forty grand. Very odd, no? But I suppose I seem to have some sort of eye, as they say, though my taste has always been just too eccentric and unfashionable for my own good."

This kind of talk made me want to sharpen knives; I didn't get enough compliments myself to bear with good grace other people's bestowing them upon themselves, but you had to play

along. Jem understood this better than I, that you could treat
people to the most lavish catalog of insults, the most fanatical
distortions of character, as long as you were willing to talk to
them about themselves, and self-understanding proved so
sketchy and vanity so filled in, that even the most puffed up
were titillated by the liberties you took.

"Who were you having dinner with tonight?" Jem asked
suddenly.

"What? No one."

"Who were you supposed to be having dinner with, and
didn't?"

"No one. What is this?"

"Why didn't you come to Oxford then, when I asked you?"

"I felt like staying home."

Jem reflected. "I can't bear to think that there is *anything*
you would rather do than be with me," he said finally. "So I
came to find out what it was."

I dug my face into his shoulder, mostly so he couldn't see
how cold my eyes were. I didn't like his putting all his cards
on the table; I felt only uncomfortable when I saw him pitiful.

"I feel like stealing tonight," he murmured. "But what's still
open in this claptrap of a one-horse town?"

"I guess you could hold up a fish-and-chips store."

"Oh God, why isn't anything twenty-four hours a day but
sickness and loneliness and craziness?"

He was stretched out now, and I put his head in my lap,
gingerly, and sang "Surabaya Johnny" to him because he liked
my flat voice.

"I won't be greedy anymore," Jem twisted himself around
to say. "Only about you."

Seven

≋

No more escorts. I would run up the stairs of Belbroughton Road and go straight to the closet. "Where's Patrick? Where have you got Andrew stashed away? Under the bed?"

No more debutantes. No more Mrs. Shaw.

At home, my father demanded little. He was often in Europe or America, and his time in England was spent going to provincial sales, hunting down pictures from houses on the block, and every weekend he stayed with friends in the country. It was an overstuffed and crumbling world he belonged to in England, cozy, knowledgeable, self-perpetuating, altogether different from the stilted and vicious expatriates he courted in New York. It was the difference between old school friends and fellow tax exiles, between family and business.

Daddy liked guests who could entertain themselves: being home at a civilized hour meant not being home at all. He didn't seem to care how often I showed up, as long as when I did, my face was clean and my manners graceful. When I was feeling neither clean nor graceful I was at the Chasms'.

I set up camp in Lupita's old room. It had a condemned look to it which suited me: a trundle bed and a child's white dresser with round knobs. Through the wall in the early morning I could hear isolated twangs from Casimir's mandolin—a groggy aubade.

Casimir had broken up with the waitress all of his own volition and was come home. Asia, the parrot, who used to bite him awake in the morning, was long dead. Mange or pip, or whatever—bile in the blood, bullet through the brain—finally picks off those cranky survivors.

We had been gambling downstairs. Jem was losing. He never lost, and it gave the game a blighted, backhanded cast. He tried to wrest the house-in-flames card from Casimir. It brought him luck.

"It brought me you," he said, unsmiling.

"Oh, nonsense, I came to you on my own steam."

"I brought her to you," reminded Casimir. We both stared. It seemed like so long ago.

"You didn't like me when you came," Jem said to me.

"You are the boy we all love to hate," said Casimir.

The front door started a hair-raising rattle, a jiggle of the bell.

"Police," said Jem. We felt like the three little pigs when the door opened and Professor Chasm came in with his stiff-legged mongrel stoop. He bent over to kiss me. "Hello, jail-bait, how are you?" Kept a hand on my backside as he glared shortsightedly at the boys, who had jumped to attention. Leaned over and shook hands.

"I didn't know you were all such pals. Don't you know any nice boys, slim? Hasn't your daddy got any more eligible clients?"

He had come back from a conference in Madrid.

"Why didn't you tell me you were going to Spain, you old ass?" Casimir demanded. "I desperately want a toreador's suit."

"You wouldn't fit into one any more than you would fit into an organ grinder's monkey suit."

Casimir grumbled.

"I must say, sweets, you haven't got much flesh on you," Professor Chasm told me.

"Jem always tells me I'm fat."

He took my skin between his fingers. "Why, you've got no more bottom than a chicken."

"Or than you."

"Well, I eat like a swine. But I drink it off, I suppose."

"Now I don't understand fashion, unlike these boys here. Why can't girls be heftier? I wish people would remember that anorexia is a disease and not what the women's magazines call an attractive accessory."

Jem got up to go.

"Jemima, where are you off to?"

"I'm getting you a drink," from between clenched teeth.

"I haven't asked for one yet. You think I'm an old soak, do you?"

"I thought you needed loosening up," said Jem, sardonically.

"He's right—I'm frightfully shy in company, really. Oh damn it all, I forgot that the boy was anorexic, too. Is that how I offended him?" he demanded gleefully.

"No. Jem's not, anymore," said Casimir. "He used to ask for an ice-cream sundae without the ice cream in grand restaurants, for an entrée. Just a bowl of caramel sauce with nuts on the side, please. No whipped cream. But now he eats the ice cream, too."

"Then what is he so touchy about?"

"He doesn't like you mauling his guests," Casimir ventured.

"Well, I reckoned that I wasn't exactly beating his time."

"Oh Daddy," said Casimir, "shut up!"

Jem was back and slammed down a mammoth whiskey

and soda before his father. "When I am mixing the drinks you had best be careful, because I keep the ground glass on ice."

"Darling boy," the Professor said, "your métier is as a barman. I always prefer the dour ones to the kind who chatter while you drink."

The Professor had fallen out once again with his battered floozy and effected a splendid reconciliation with his wife, inviting her home with all forgiven. I had developed a soft spot for Stephanie, who made herself at home in this can of worms and now channeled into homemaking an ardor that might otherwise have been spent on more radical causes. But Jem found hard to stomach the new burst of togetherness which embraced the boys as well. It was like a borstal, he said pettishly, clotted stews doled out of pots like mass graves, and once Stephanie had gone so far as to venture upstairs with a vacuum.

Without explanation, Jem moved to our flat in London. He was circumspect around Daddy: he wore black brogues instead of basketball sneakers and knotted his tie with a knot the size of a hazelnut. Each evening he gave my father eight minutes of his time and no more. It was an audience, all right. He dished up for Daddy a few choice *trouvailles* from his magpie's nest of curiosities. Being a boy who lived in *Guides Bleus*, he could reel off like a tour guide the contents of every provincial museum in Europe but in a tone as flat as Kansas, and when he was done he retired to my bedroom to smoke and play his latest New Wave recording. Daddy didn't like loud music or cigarettes and didn't like boys in girls' rooms. He referred to Jem as the spook and the undertaker. He was angling for provocation, a breach for which he could thoroughly lambaste him. And Jem was forcing Daddy's hand. I should have told him not to come, but I couldn't. I was like a bee drowning in the sweetness of these nights, when Jem would

sprawl across the bed with his head in my lap, reading aloud
to me and telling me stories. God, I loved him so much those
days: I used to count all his fingers and toes like a newborn
baby. And it made me hold him tighter for those hours when
I didn't know where he was going when he went—always a
little after midnight, and after the last train to Oxford had left.
He was so black these days all I could be sure was that he was
doing himself wrong. I tried to tell him once that when you're
loved, certain rights to do yourself dirt are no longer yours,
but he wanted every freedom to himself, he shrugged it all off.
He said that pain was good for me too: it was the only teacher.
I didn't believe it; it sounded like sentimental foolishness. The
only teacher—well, I'd learned already not to be a malcontent. How many times did I need to learn that lesson over in
order to be human? But pain was a thicker book than that, he
said; always more lessons than one had learned. You could go
deeper and deeper and still there was no end to it. I was only
at the skin of it, the flinching surface. If I wanted to be with
him, we had to meet in hell. I didn't know if I had the faith
to go that far without drawing back. You could get to hell and
even then you weren't certain of bringing your baby back.

I never knew which way he would turn. Sometimes he
would twist around and grab me, hold me tight and say, con-
solingly, "What's wrong, honey, what's wrong, pet? Don't
tremble. Everything's going to be all right; we'll all die happy."

And sometimes when he saw how scared I was, he would
get angry, tell me I asked too much of him and gave nothing.
I was very frightened all the time of his dying on me.

When the breach came I wasn't even there to see it. Daddy
walked into my bedroom one evening and saw Jem propped
up in bed stripped to the waist, reading a railway guide to
Eastern Europe (we were planning to go to Prague) and eating
chocolate. Where was I? At the piano recital with Mrs. Pala-

fox. There was a dustup. Jem didn't stand up when my father came in. Jem was insolent. When I got home, Jem had left and my father was licking his wounds.

"I cannot say I think much of the company you keep, Jezebel," Daddy remarked, drumming his nails against the kitchen counter.

"What are you saying?"

"I'm talking about that boy, who I believe is one of the most unpleasant characters I've encountered. I didn't want to say anything at first—after all, he's Charlie's son and I thought, well, perhaps the boy has simply got rather unfortunate manners. But darling, the creature is not only charmless, he's a menace. I'm not a bit happy about your running about with that thug."

I had begun busying myself with the sole of my shoe, exploring tenderly the beginnings of a leak.

"Darling, one of the reasons I didn't fight harder to wrest you away from your poor eccentric old mother is that young people in London seemed so pathetic and destructive. All these horrid cheap drugs that get bandied about, all this self-mutilation that goes on in the name of fashion. I wanted you to preserve a little innocence and common sense, to stay a child for a decent interval. I thought you would be safer growing up in New York."

"Daddy, I don't take drugs."

"Darling, believe it or not, I trust in your good sense. But people will think you do, gadding about with that maundering granny-basher, and that is almost as bad. I don't consider that sad young man worth losing your reputation for."

Daddy was the second person to say that. The first had been Casimir.

"Is that all?"

"Jezebel, I shudder to think what your ma lets you do all

year round, but for the month or so I've got you in my clutches—and I don't ask much—you must try to toe the line a *bit*. I'd just as soon you kept a little distance between yourself and that young man."

"You want me not to hang around with Jem?" I thought it over. "I can't say that I'll do that, Daddy."

"I'd like to know why not."

"I just can't."

"Have you made some kind of foolish promise?"

"Just my heart and soul," I answered, on the edge of laughter. It sounded so maudlin.

"My dear, I can tell you this much: A heart is much easier to regain than a reputation."

Now I laughed outright.

"You've got such a sweet smile, my angel. I do wish you would take care of your appearance."

I looked down at myself: a pair of cotton pajamas, a boy's striped T-shirt, flat espadrilles which I half kicked off as I walked. Shiftless. My toilette consisted of soap and water and a change of clothes every morning. Let my looks look after themselves. I wanted my father to say that I was pretty, but all he said in a governessy voice was, "You've got good posture which is half the battle. If you simply *dressed*, instead of scuffing around like a whipped dog . . . Now Clothilde, for instance, is ugly as sin, but she pulls herself together to look like a million bucks. I do wish you'd let her take you shopping one afternoon. The point, sweet pea, is self-esteem. You don't *need* to hang around with that damaged and hopeless creature. You're better quality than that, and you should have higher expectations."

He wanted to be able to show me off. "I want to be so proud of you," he said. I didn't listen to the rest, because I knew it was too late; that if he was going to put some care into me, it would have to have been done a long time back.

Because now I only wanted to be quality goods to make a better present of myself to Jem.

The next morning Daddy cooked breakfast for the two of us. We usually stuck to a walking black coffee as we dressed— Daddy was a late sleeper for a grown man, and I didn't like to eat. But this morning I sat down to a set place bearing a whole family of fried eggs and strips of bacon laid out like corpses with their toes in the air.

He had spoken already to Mrs. Palafox this morning, he told me, who would be thrilled to bits to take me to South Moulton Street that afternoon to nose around. "'I hope nosing is all you do,' I told her. I fear for my fortune in the hands of such a hardened profligate as old Clo."

I rearranged my plate. Yellow eggs and pink bacon. Pink bacon and yellow eggs.

"I can't go this afternoon," I said. "I'm going to Oxford to see Jem."

He clearly wished I hadn't said it. He didn't know what to answer. "It's on your own head, sweetheart," was all my father said.

I flew for the next train from Paddington. It was easier moving than reflecting, but in vain I posed for pictures in the photo booth and gorged myself on British Rail biscuits, read other people's newspapers sideways and quarreled with the conductor.

While the slow train jiggled and creaked from Cholmsley to Wolmsley to Moulmsley—the road to hell is paved with market towns—when I was feeling too queasy to spy on any more newspapers, then there was no recourse but to think of what had been done and what was to come, and dread and remorse made me hungry for Jem.

"Sweetheart." I was draped around him. I wasn't going to let go.

"You're rather quixotic lately, Scarlet." Jem, in his pajama bottoms, still scalded and dripping from a bath with no cold water, was trying to put an espresso pot in the sink, but I was hugging him too hard for him to move.

"You think I don't love you because I've been so vile," I said.

"I thought you told me recently love was a word that wasn't in your dictionary."

"You know I love you."

"Well, Jezebel, love is a wonderful thing, but if you don't let me go get a shave, people are going to think it's abduction by an Albanian bandit." And he seared my cheek with the stubble of his blue chin.

Jem was the most desperate soul I knew to hear what people said about him. (And then what? And then what? What did he mean by that? Is that all?) Today, his refusal to ask what had happened after he left, to show surprise at my turning up unannounced at eleven on a Monday morning, made melodrama impossible. He sensed that such trouble was coming, he could only play it down, only resort to the rigid machinery of routine.

Every morning Jem went to an Italian barbershop on Queen Street. Casimir and I were dragged along sometimes to watch. The barber was in love with Casimir, and while Jem was trussed up in white drapery to the chin, Domenico's eyes wandered wistfully to Casimir, the straight razor at Jem's throat. He ritually pulled Casimir's black curls as we walked out, asking, "When am I going to get to cut this?"

Jem scuffed on the white basketball sneakers I had brought him from America. Black T-shirt and a black blazer. Casimir, coming down the stairs, cast him a look of great disgust.

"Are you wearing your pajamas outside? This is too frightful, what will Domenico think?"

"He'll think I couldn't keep away a minute longer. And I

can't. Anyway, if Jezebel can catch a train in her pajamas, surely I can get a shave in mine. Shall we go?"

Trying to get someplace with Jem and Casimir was like being an imperiled buffer zone. Jem moved like a hummingbird that dies if it stays still, bundling me into clothes and taxis. "Hold your horses," said Casimir. Departure was a threatening word. Barring our departure were a few Marlboros to be smoked, a shot of white rum waiting to be funneled into Coca-Cola and sipped, a story about a customs official in Rangoon and another about a cat house in Bombay. He liked to hold everyone in suspension to watch him take his time. Jem was in blue jeans by the time we left.

Jem pranced down the Banbury Road ahead of us, continually doubling back like a kite on a string, recalled. Dazzling day. Chiseled clouds. Graven sun. Jem was feeling like a caper. Ominous sign—his capers always ended in broken bits. He would butt the chandelier with his head until a crystal came crashing down, he would take a mask off the wall and do a war dance behind it until the whiskers fell off. He was death to anything inflammable, anything fragile, anything that went by clockwork.

"I got a present for you," Domenico told Casimir excitedly. "Last night I went to the Phoenix: a film by this chap Cocteau, and the boys all had their hair like—well, I'll show you how."

"Which film?" asked Casimir suspiciously as he moved into the red plastic chair.

"A Cocteau film. Haven't you been to school? *Coc*-teau. High-class."

"He can only mean the black leather motorcyclists in *Orphée*," said Jem. "Hey, Domenico, why can't I have a haircut like that too?"

"No, this is for Casimir. You—you haven't got enough hair."

But when Casimir emerged, long curls flopping in his eyes and the back of his head shaved, it was *Les Enfants Terribles* and not the angels of death that had inspired Domenico.

"I dunno," he said with a modest shrug. "It reminded me of you kids, somehow."

Outside the shop, Casimir grabbed Jem by the throat, pulling out his flick knife. "I got a present for you, Orpheus. You want a haircut, too, hmmm?" He started sawing at a lock of Jem's hair.

"I thought a Coctelian poodle's topknot might suit you. How about a pair of flannel shorts and school satchel?" And Jem disengaged himself. "Now to the market."

Shopping always gave me a chill, recalling department store Santa Clauses and getting lost in the lingerie. But under Jem's manipulation it was different. He drew up magnificent and quirky lists and walked me quickly through each station, not letting me dawdle. The shopkeepers of the covered market, with its aisles of salamis and brocades, loathed Jem. He bargained and often didn't buy; imaginary ballrooms and dinner parties were outfitted there, while he haggled as if he were in an Istanbul bazaar. It was his fantasy, but their livelihood.

But today Jem was docile, fingering cut tulips, while Casimir bought provisions at Palms. I was so used to Jem dancing around me, snapping at my heels, that I was oblivious to his haranguing by now. I knew that the favorite in his orbit would always be the villain, someone to contradict and whiplash, and I didn't mind being called vacant or sullen when I ignored him. But that day he treated me to a rather haunting solicitousness. The night before was not mentioned, but he kept me by his side with a watchfulness that electrified me, and held my arm like a police escort, like a partner at the ball. Once only he scampered away, and was back an instant later with a packet of White Cardinal snuff.

"You see, my snorts, at least, are in deference to the Holy

Roman Church. Jiggle a pinch onto the back of your hand. In Mexican marketplaces you can get snuff along with other heaps of spices in newspaper cones. It's sloppier than these sterilized tins, but one feels like such a bandit for one's pains." He wiped my nose with his handerchief. "There's a don at Christ Church whose handkerchief is one brown splotch from the stuff. It's a repulsive habit, but it makes you devilishly clearheaded. Well, isn't it worth dribbling black snot for a level head?"

"I feel a little itchy today," Casimir ventured. "How about a stealing spree?"

"I want to steal a black Mercedes and drive it to the coast," said Jem.

"What coast—Bournemouth?" I grimaced.

"Newhaven. Dieppe. Across the Pyrenees to Gibraltar and across the straits. Tunisia."

We went to Woolworth's by default. I liked watching masters at work, and Jem was a master thief, a performer whose clean rapacity craved cameras and store detectives. We had our photographs taken—my second set for the day. Then Jem stuffed down his shirt front alarm clocks, music box ballerinas, African violets. At the end, he bought a chocolate bar and we left.

Casimir's eyes narrowed, blowing smoke at the lens. Casimir a drooping Pierrot and me with round eyes and tremulous mouth. The back of Casimir's head. Jem and I huddled together, Casimir grinning.

Passing the hospital beyond St. Giles, Jem strolled into the foyer. The receptionist stared as he emptied his bulging shirt front onto the counter. "Will you please distribute these among the patients who are bored?"

We had a picnic late that afternoon on the fire escape at Belbroughton Road. That fire escape was an innovation the Professor had insisted upon. "Else you boys will broil in your beds if the fumes of those cheap cigars you smoke don't smother you first."

But so far the fire escape had been used only as dining room or quick-escape hatch. The boys were both jealous of each other's moves: if Jem suspected Casimir of being in a hurry to get someplace Jem didn't know about, he would tease Casimir with long good-byes and suddenly urgent stories, big kisses on both cheeks. They were the only boys I knew who kissed each other every morning and at night before they went to bed.

"What's the plunder?" Jem demanded. Casimir had bought a loaf of bread, a moldering monument of Gorgonzola, a slag heap of coffee beans, slabs of black chocolate. We opened a bottle of champagne and reclined on the cast iron in the dying heat of the day, spitting satsuma seeds at the squirrels and the few passersby.

Jem resumed his besotted attentiveness to me in the unspoken ways one does—by staring at me, by making canards of bread and chocolate for me, by feeding me thimblefuls of champagne from silver foil glasses he had molded from the chocolate wrapper.

It was staying light in the evenings and we felt that keen exhilaration of emerging at last from pitch-black days. Before nightfall we walked through the long grasses of the university parks all the way to Addison's Walk, where the Cherwell had flooded its banks from the downpours of that month. Ducks were floating in the middle of what used to be meadow.

I stayed that night. I don't think there was any question of my going home. We stayed up and stayed up, not wanting to go to bed until the dawn came and sparrows started chattering and the business of living was begun again. Once I drew back the ballroom curtain, half expecting to see Mrs. Shaw waiting for Jem: a thin black figure with eyes downcast, standing in the lamplight which cast a moon path over the pavement as upon a black, black sea. But there was no one there, no death-announcing raven, no silent banshee. Only dons and their wives coming home from the theater.

"You could always come and live here. It's not very luxurious but there's plenty to eat," said Jem.

"I suppose I'd have to make my living."

"You could be a gardener's apprentice in the Botanical Gardens," Casimir said. "You could gag the Alsatian and let Jem steal all the tulips."

"There is no Alsatian," said Jem. "It's what the watchman says to clear people out quickly at closing time. Anyway, you wouldn't have to work. I'd take care of you."

We climbed out again onto the fire escape, when its scaffolding was so very black against the pinks and grays of early morning. Till it grows pink outside and the champagne dribbles through the door, I said to myself. I thought about the scene awaiting me at home in a few hours, and it made the air sweeter and keener. Eustacius used to say when I fretted, "Don't you tremble about them parrots and them gaudies. Just you keep your head high, high like ship prow."

I ducked my head and let the breakers roll over me and crash.

"My darling, I am a working man. I cannot guard you night and day. I thought you had enough sense, after our conversation, not to flout me deliberately. I ask so very little of you, after all. Perhaps too little. But if you find that young man so irresistible, you can see him on your own steam."

That meant money and protection. But it didn't mean that; it meant that I was booked for a plane back to New York, and that Mummy was expecting me on the thirtieth of July.

"Don't be hangdog, Jezebel. You asked for it. And it won't be so dismal; New York in the summer is rather jolly, I've always thought. Big, empty streets and all the smart shops *en solde*. It isn't a punishment. And you're extremely fortunate that Mrs. Palafox has taken such a fancy to you. She has told me already that she expects you to come and stay with her on Long Island often."

And so I had to call Jem and tell him I was leaving in a week. I hated the telephone. I hated the urgent din it made if you took it off the hook. I hated ringing and not knowing who would answer and whether you would have to give your name or not. I hated people's muted or blaring telephone voices, the static shuffling and squirming while they got into position for a real long chat.

Well, Jem wasn't a chatterer. He sounded dull and child-like, uninterested.

"Jem, will you come say good-bye?"

"No."

"Oh. Shall I come to Oxford, then?"

"No. Stay tight, if you can." And then, after a long silence, "I'll try to work something out." But when I telephoned again, five days later, it was Stephanie who answered and told me that Jem was gone.

Her name—what was it? Brunhilde or Ermintrude. Something you might name a big doll. Jem called her nothing but Mrs. Shaw. But I saw her name once, printed on a Coutts check across which raced a desperate misspelled message for Jem in a Frenchified hand. And once again, having my hair cut, in an old *House & Garden* which featured the Belgravia Mews house of Mrs. Geoffrey Shaw. Curled up in a mound of cushions was a pale caramel-colored Mongol with paler lipstick and paler still hair, lacquered into a bouffant. That blond pallor that makes coloring look vulgar. She knew how to pose: plucked eyebrows lifted in an expression of surprise. The pho-

tographs, crammed with gleaming expanses of crystal and silver, made it tougher to imagine Jem with his basketball sneakers on the leopardskin rug, asking for a can of Coca-Cola.
Svetlana?

I dreamed about her—that she was dying and wanted me
to give Jem back. When I woke up, I wasn't jealous anymore.
I wanted Jem to be seeing her again.

Casimir came over Sunday morning, the day before I left for
New York, and deposited a bunch of black grapes in my lap.

"I'd like to take you to Spain, where these came from. I
didn't get the pipless ones—I always feel lost without something to spit."

Sometimes it was easier to be happy with Casimir than
Jem.

"I'm going to take you out today. Let's get drunk and feed
the swans grapes," he said. He was wearing outing clothes: a
dusty pink linen jacket, pink-and-white striped seersucker
trousers, and white suede shoes. We went to that bower of
tropical storms the Beachcomber, where every Malay barman
was a special pal of Casimir's, and we downed Singapore slings
in the luminous dark. Casimir fished out a gardenia for his
buttonhole and pinned another, gin-soaked, in my hair.
When we had run out of cash and credit, we went to St.
James's Park and took a boat out on the lake.

"Where is Mrs. Shaw?" I asked Casimir, as he circumnavi-
gated us top-speed between boats crammed with babies and
dogs and ice cream.

"On ice," he said gaily.

"Jem isn't with her?"

"He doesn't need to be. She's his squaw, she's waiting for
him."

"But he should see her."

"He's seeing you. He can't concentrate on two people at once. All he talks about is you."

"But he's gone. Where is he now?"

"I expect he's with her," said Casimir inconsistently.

The same kind of seeming insensibility that masked Casimir's alert malice and lulled people into telling him everything made it possible for him to deliver such stomach drops with utter unconcern. I discounted Jem's attempts to agonize me more than he himself was agonized, but Casimir's casual revelations were fatal in their disinterest.

So Jem had moved in with Mrs. Shaw before I had even left the country. That white slug.

Between strokes. Black water. White swans. Black grapes. We drifted.

"What does he say about me? All we do is fight. We don't even *like* each other. In fact, I hate his puling guts."

"Well, what do you suppose he and Mama did all day? Jem carries on these days like a bereft turtledove, but Christ, I didn't care to be in the middle of *that* dogfight."

The grapes sank to the bottom like bullets when we tried to feed the swans, so we spat seeds at them instead.

"Mummy would say, 'For heaven's sake, boy, that nasal whine, I cannot *bear*. *Who* taught you to talk through your nose? I didn't. It was that American school. Wanna, gotta—pfui.' And Jem would tell her that her dress was unbecoming, that her breasts were too sagging to wear such a décolletage. 'If I don't dress you down to the shoe buckles, you appear like a tart in a gold rush town.'"

Casimir spat with vicious aim, *ping* at the swan's fanfare of gleaming feather.

"Watch it," I warned. "They beat people up."

"But perhaps the most revolting sight of all was their dinners. When the cancer had eaten up her insides Jem would compete with Mama to eat less than she. You should have seen them toying with their food. If Jemmy relented and swallowed a mouthful or two, he would immediately go and make himself be sick. They went for the jugular all right, those two, and the rest of the time was spent soothing each other's wounded nerves."

Snarling and charming: I knew the formula.

"But anyway," said Casimir dismissively, "I don't know where Jem is. He's gone off on a sulk."

Spain or the Europa Motel? I wondered. It wouldn't do to fret before Casimir, who was already telling me he was going to get me a black cygnet for my birthday.

Eight

≈≈≈

The highway was jammed from the airport to town. The bumper to bumper traffic's blare and the radio merged into a siren song luring me from my destination.

The radio advertised a course for croupiers at the School of Casino Management: instruction in how to deal a mean game of crap, baccarat, blackjack. How to spin the wheel of chance. The radio advertised a school of bartending: how to mix anything from a pink lady to a pousse-café. Both courses implied that their graduates would get more dates than they'd ever had before. The radio advertised a search conducted by *Velvet* magazine for the most desirable woman in the world, price twenty grand. But you had to be twenty-one to be a bartender or a croupier or even the world's most desirable woman, and I was only nineteen.

I closed my eyes until we hit the Triborough Bridge and that vertical island posed its profile, all at once, chin up, and by the time the taxi driver was unloading my suitcases on the sidewalk at Ninety-fourth Street, and I saw Mummy swaying welcomes at the top of the steps in a poppy-embroidered dressing gown, I had moved from England to New York.

Truly the gap was Eustacius's great divide, stripping the live and waking from the dead and mad. Once inside the front door, I was a goner. For in New York I never ventured outside the house: everything beloved, every dark and thick and rich fetish, every rum and coconut paradise lay within. England was my New World, all expanse of surface to be sounded. But in New York I could not stray—every object gone to seed, springs broken, contained properties of long association. The fresh-as-paint bloom of America had been overblown, and it was the seediness that lingered. New York was an old city, born old: barberships in which depression-old tobacco droppings were steeped in the cracks of the leather swivel chairs like hundred-year tea; restaurants which hadn't taken down the Christmas decorations from the year the war ended. And my house a drafty memento mori for the already dead. The nodding mandarin on the lacquered table hadn't nodded since Aunt Celestine and my mother were little girls. (My grandmother settled disputes with the Chinaman: its bowing ceased when the head was inclined in Celestine's direction. She had her way. But once, when their father was made judge, Mummy won. And Celestine bashed the Chinaman over my mother's head.) And the black and gold lacquer table on which the broken mandarin sat had replaced the peacock-feathered table because the feathers brought bad luck.

The kitchen sink was always stuffed with fresh flowers while the flowers in vases throughout the rooms were stiff and dead. The fumes of festering flowers mingled with scents of crumbling leather, rum, and wet fur were the scent of New York for me.

The house was pitch black and shaking and crashing to the blare of *Trovatore*. There was guttering candlelight in the dining room where Mummy had made herself a lair on the leopardskin rug to wait up for me. A glass overturned when she heard the taxi pull up, a handful of flowers that had resisted her arrangements scattered. I was meant to sit upright at the table where Eustacius had laid a place for me, with my steamship mug painted Jezebel in stars, and an offering like birthday party favors: the letters that had come while I was gone and two odd-shaped packets in purple tissue paper and gold ribbon. The bigger one, torn apart, was an ivory cross from the West Indies traced pink in henna and bound by silver twine.

"Honestly, I get so worried about you crossing all those waters, and since the Pope devalued St. Christopher, I guess you can only trust in Jesus," said Mummy apologetically. The littler lumpy parcel was a handful of glass marbles. "I remembered how you were always so good at those." It was a sinister memory. I was nearly thrown out of school when I was little for beating up all the girls in my class who wouldn't lose their marbles honestly, and snatching their collections anyway. The mothers banded together to complain, until Mummy was asked to come in to school and discuss my problem. She never did, and I guess they decided I had bigger problems.

Once she had fed me the cold soup Eustacius had left, Mummy didn't know what to do with me. The formulas of "Why don't you just go straight to bed?" or "Wouldn't you like a nice cool bath?" hung in the air just beyond reach. I guess she knew that I had been bad or she would have asked as she always did after her favorite J. I was all strung up with longing to hear his name on this side of the abyss, but all she ventured was, "I must say I wish Casimir would come to New York again."

"Casimir," I repeated in disgust. "Why Casimir, in God's name?"

"And teach Eustacius math. My poor old accountant just keeled over, and his successor is too wily by half. I want Eustacius to learn to do the taxes for us."

"But Mummy, he still can't read or write, can he?"

"Oh, there's no reading or writing: it's all numbers. And Eustacius really picks up everything so fast. I was telling him about crème brûlée the other day and he understood before the words were out of my mouth how you'd keep the sugar crust light enough so's it wouldn't sink. He's smart as a whip."

"Anyway, why Casimir?"

"Isn't that what he studies—math?"

She had dredged up from God knows what depths a tall tale with which Casimir had regaled us on his visit to New York several years ago of a postgraduate mathematics lecture he had delivered at the university when a don he had gone boozing with the night before had too bad a hangover to perform.

"Mummy, Casimir's just a wag. Anyway, you don't need a mathematician to do your taxes. Why don't you get another accountant?"

She was gazing at me strangely, in an inspired sort of way. "Don't you—don't you—sweetie, wouldn't you like a nice bath before you go to bed?"

I was in the West Indian fourposter bed with the curtains drawn about, the mosquito netting a shining cocoon. A million malarial mosquitoes and dull moths could batter themselves against the gauzed whiteness, but there I was safe. A little bit safe, as long as I didn't come out. As long as I didn't even speak. Morning can be the darkest pit. When you don't know what to do with yourself all day until it's time to sneak back to bed again, when the prospect of so many more years of living appalls. It seemed as if every lady in my family had always stayed in bed all day. I wondered, were there ladies who got up for lunch, for breakfast? If you went to Pullman cars for breakfasttime, or to hotel dining rooms, would there be ladies there who had chosen not to order a tray to their bedsides? Might there be one or two among all the men and the empty tables in white linen and pink carnations? Mrs. Palafox didn't rise for lunch, and the same example had been set for me. My skirmishes, decidedly, were to be set among the bed-clothes. I thought of all the people who had lived in my bed before me, and of how difficult they had found it even to dangle their feet over the edge. Bourbon-voiced Thadée Dablevert, who had brought the bed back to Cocodrie from Domenica, and got five mulatto children in it by his cook Quivive: Zeferin, Tobago and Flor, Zamora, Deuteronomie. He thought the grand Creoles in Louisiana were duds: I guess they thought him a little tacky too. In those days if you didn't like where you lived, you lived in the Sears Roebuck catalog, and in the Bible, and in bed. No nonsense about exercise. I had the Dablevert Bible, too. Thadée used to make those yellow children crawl on their knees across the room to his bed, so he could belabor them about the backside with the Holy Scriptures until they were grateful for his bounty in letting them be half-white. A Bible-loving man. But what the children didn't realize, or Quivive either, perhaps until Thadée died, was that the Bible was hollowed, and inside no Isaiah or Ecclesiastes, but a silver flask initialed TGD, which to this day stinks dankly of old bourbon. They thought they were getting a walloping from the Hand of Fate, but instead it was plain old Beelzebub!

No, I wouldn't get out of bed because, really, there was no call to.

I thought about the century of dust hanging above me, sinking the canopies lower: dust that even long-handled bamboo feather dusters wouldn't dislodge. I felt that any moment the canopy might burst from the weight of all that dust, covering me in a mountain like those inhabitants of Arabia Bishop Taylor was so sad about.

"Jezebel, what you doing in there?"

"Eustacius, I'm just resting."

"You got no call to rest any more. It's almost twelve o'clock and you breakfast going to get up and walk away. I ain't fixing to have another child in the house lazy as you mother. You get up and put on some slippers now."

Yes, things were certainly getting bad. You weren't even safe in your own bed any more what with all the dust and the disturbances.

I kissed Eustacius's scrapply-smelling cheek. Every time I saw him he had got smaller. "How are you, Eustacius?"

"I still here. How's Jezebel?"

"I missed you. I get into bad ways when you're not around."

"Oh, I still around."

"How are all your girl friends?" Eustacius was the only civilized one among us: he knew all the neighbors, and had everyone's maids and cooks over for parties that went on all night. (He and his bossy righteousness.)

"They up to no good—Viola and her monkey business." Eustacius shook his head. "My goodness, she always up to something. I miss that Georgie who used to be with Mrs. Bishop—she went back to Nashville where her daughter-in-law could look after her. Her heart just skipped a beat too many, but my she was a fine dancer. Mrs. Bishop sure was sorry to lose Georgie, too. Where you slippers? You don't come into my kitchen with no shoes on. You a grown lady now."

Eustacius wouldn't let me eat in the kitchen either, but sat me in the dining room, all purple satin in daylight like a Mexican funeral. So cold the butter on the waffles wouldn't melt. Those were the compensations for being a lady and for a lost Jem. Cold butter and plum-colored satin.

. . .

I dreamed that I was in a hospital in the tropics. Jem and I were lying side by side in a bed swathed in mosquito netting, in a long corridor of white cots. Wide shuttered doors, baby-blue walls, conventual furniture. It was a French mission in Indochina. The sisters came and told us we had a visitor. A Mr. Jem was here to see us. I tried to explain that it could not be—this was Jem right beside me, and anyway nobody knew we were here; nobody could possibly know. The sisters wouldn't listen, and I appealed to Jem, but he wasn't moving. Then I could see a man coming all the way down the corridor, and he was brilliant as Madama Butterfly in fluttering colors. He came and sat down beside our bed and he had no head upon his shoulders. I wondered how I could talk to him if he had no head, and I was sure Jem knew, but he still wasn't moving, and I was frightened that if I whispered to Jem that the man had no head, he would be angry.

I wish I could write about fruit trees and dirt roads and muddy rivers rushing their banks. But here it is New York City, the Year of Our Lord 1980, and a summer when the most ornery heat waged war with sudden downpours, and it thundered mutinously. One went about groggy during the day and sleepless at night. Waiting for the weather to break. Me, I was waiting for anything to break—my heart intolerably strong, my body cheap durable stuff like cotton. How could you preach about dust and mutability when you begged your body to break and it gave back sunny health, stretches of seemly flesh punctuated with dimples, ripening with a low hum; not a bruise, not a tear in the skin to show for all the inner rendings, when if the soul were a coil of rope it would be gnawed in two by now.

The shaft confounds, not that it wounds, sings Pandarus of love, Pandarus who wants to keep things light and comely,

Pandarus the doctor whose intimate art only prolongs that long disease life. Whoever died of love? No one did. (Yes, I felt like false Cressida for skipping out on my baby, and had I turned tail with every Greek in camp I could not have felt more forsworn.) I was searching hard each minute of the day to place Jem, running my hands over his soap, his cigars, his linen, his books, his newspapers. What flowers? What ink? What light of the sky? What was let in the gates of that besieged city, his body? White or black angels? Innocent things, milk, bread and butter, or was it only those demons of concentration, black coffee, black tobacco? My mind reeled like a compass that couldn't find its north, its south.

"Eustacius, do you ever feel like there's so much time swamping ahead of you before you can lie down in peace, that you just want to blast the whole gulf of it to kingdom come?"

"No, honey, I don't figure I got all *that* much time left, but I pretty happy with what I got. I don't know how old I *is*, but I older than this century and I sure don't count on laying eyes on the next one."

"Oh, don't die, Eustacius."

"Oh, honey, when you as old as me you don't die. The tide just so low you walk out into the water and keep on walking out."

But something had fallen flat because I could only stay indoors out of the heat, and stare, glazed, at scraps of paper covered in his terrible green writing. The foul invader had pitched camp in my heart; an unnamable whine, a bile of the blood.

I was frightened to take a bath, especially in the morning when the blackness hit the worst. And then I got too frightened to sleep at night, and too jumpy to turn on the light. I made Jem command in my head, "You just melt," but sounds made me sit bolt upright in the dark and question the prowlers.

Why . . . why . . . why. . . . Do not ask. Why do sinners' ways prosper, Lord? Why do birds sing so gay, why do the heathen rage? When a dead house chatters to perdition, why does it have no front door? When I haven't two cents to knock together for the clash that keeps the beasts at bay, how do I strike gold? This is panic fear, this, the dark. The morning comes without light, but only rancorous, hung-over boredom which drags its feet from room to room of an unkempt house, which sprawls flat on its stomach in the afternoon, in a faded kimono, turning over blank pages. When I cannot move because it is all I can do to hold on tight and ballast my insides against the falling, falling.

When we were alone, Mummy said with inexhaustible good nature, "Tell me what's on your mind, dumpling. You'll feel better for getting it out of your system. Curse me out if it would make you feel better. Just don't bottle it up."

But how could you bottle up nothing? Nothing was what I was butting my head against. Nothing was the manacles and the fetters. There was nothing under the sun, nothing as far as the eye could see, and beyond, world after world, of nothing. Sometimes I sniveled a little, sometimes I scowled. You see, it was only Jem who had finally got me to talk, and when he left, he took his bag of tricks with him. Before, I could hold inspired conversations in my head, but face to face it had always been pictures on the floor traced with the toe of my shoe, and silences that extended to deserts without oases. It was only Jem whose talk had made words rise to the tongue like greedy trout the way they did in dreaming, and silences cavort like porpoises in the lucid depths of the unspoken—the unspoken no longer a burden, but possibly our future.

Eustacius was getting sharper with me, and Mummy intervened. "She's not being ornery, really, Eustacius. I'm just afraid she's beginning to take after my side of the family and not Desmond's." And that was another mistake. My father was not some pink and white trilling cockatoo, not a riveting castrato. But who? I would tell you if I knew. Maybe I was spawn of a busboy, a mulatto groom.

Eustacius, addressing me directly, said that I was coming apart at the seams. "You hair's a rat's nest. You shoes all broken and you clothes raggle-taggle." ("She's gone with the raggle-taggle gypsies-oh," went my favorite song when I was little, about a young lady who left her fine lord on a stormy night. "What care I for my silken bed? With the sheets turned down so bravely-oh? For tonight I will sleep in a cold dark field/ Along with the raggle-taggle gypsies-oh.") "Honey, the hem of you dress all coming down in back. Now you get inside you head and you do a little housekeeping inside there."

How do you tidy a ravine? How do you send darkness to the dry cleaners? Those mustard-colored children shuffling on their knees across the floor, asking their father for forgiveness for being born, were more real to me than I was. Airline hostesses advertising cheap fares in old magazines I leafed through were more real. No one was as worthless.

If I could blame something, it would be this: not knowing where Jem was. Hellishly not knowing. To have fixed him in my mind's sight on the floor of the ballroom in Belbroughton Road, occupying precisely five harlequin squares; three black, two white would have been an anchor, knowing at rock bottom there could be no further sinking.

But when I telephoned once, struck dumb with stage fright to be about to speak to Jem, it was only Casimir who told me Jem was not there anymore—he had gone away for good. Professor Chasm had entrusted him with a project, a spy mission, Casimir put it. Casimir wasn't allowed to know anything about it, but Jem had a lot of money to throw around and had then just disappeared. Jem an agent on a secret mission? It was so obvious and so unlikely. The stage properties, the talents required were so much his already that truly he could have been nothing else save the director of a finishing school for young ladies or a Vatican diplomat. But suddenly I would have rather he fester than be a free adult and clear of me. I would have felt better had he said good-bye. As you grow older, you respect those rites of passage which offend the snobbery of young people, who prefer to be thrown to the dogs or laid out on the towers of silence without all the amenities of carnations and embalmers' stage paint. But it is right to let your family take a look at you just to make sure that you are really dead. It would have been right for Jem to let me kiss him good-bye before he became a citizen, a missing person, before he grew up and walked off the edge of the world. It was a last gasp of his surly and vainglorious childishness that made him duck, without a splash.

The city now was stinking, angry, maudlin. When I went outside, wheedling men followed me, delivery boys crooned filthy sweet-talk at me, and I shook too much to confront the stir I caused in the street. The city held nothing for me but sick thoughts of loss.

Mrs. Palafox had the house by the ocean where she spent every summer, as she had with her parents as a little girl, winding up a long year's traipse across Europe. They must have been among the first summer people on Long Island— as she, like Eustacius, was something older than this century—and I envisaged them migrating from Fifth Avenue like new frontiersmen, with the chests of linen and silver strapped to the roof of the Packard, and the servants following in the train.

Then the island must have been entirely given over to waterfowl and potato farmers.

I didn't answer her telephone calls until September. She asked me to come out and stay with her. She was writing her memoirs, with which I could be a divine help.

"Of course, it will be dull as ditchwater out here—early to bed, and the ocean when you want to take a dip, and my darling old Dawkins and Mrs. Dawkins to keep us alive. The bare essentials, you understand. But you're the sole creature I know who doesn't need bright lights and Broadway."

"Sounds heaven to me." I was already picking up her celestial rapport.

"Now babykins"—her telephone voice sputtered and crackled like a bad connection—"can you drive? I'm such a city creature that without a fellow to motor me about in the old sedan I'm stranded. Maurice, that's the gardener, is too blind, and Dawkins is too old to learn. We just keep a running account at Paul's Taxi."

"I can't drive, but I guess I'm not too old."

"That's the ticket. Dawkins is such a *dope*—I tell him, 'Sweetie, it's as easy as pie. D means drive, and you give her a little juice and GO.'"

Nine

And somehow she had given me a little juice, and I went, too. So that two months after I had come home, I waded through another bon voyage breakfast—waffles and maple syrup and kidneys, and coffee hot and strong and black as love, but not as fleeting. Mummy and Eustacius were relieved to see the last of me. It felt like the first time I had dressed in two months. I felt like a released patient in my street clothes. I even managed to hail a cab and to lug my transatlantic trunk onto the Long Island Rail Road car, and I came out the other end black as a tarbaby from flattening my nose against windowpanes preserved in soot.

Mrs. Palafox in a white sailor suit and red patent leather pumps was waiting for me at the station by a lipstick-red sports car. The gardener was at the wheel. He was dead black and had only one eye, and that one was evil. I felt unexpectedly glad to see her and to hold her hand as we sat dead upright in the backseat together. She clutched me extra hard. "Close your eyes. Say, Maurice"—as the car started—"why doncha take it a little easy on the gas? Of course *my* old cast-iron stomach doesn't matter a damn, but think of fluttery lovey-dovey here."

I couldn't shut my eyes. The flat, bare land was bathed in a cold washed-out light that turned the colorlessness to crystal. She lived in a bleak shingled house in the gray-grassed dunes, on a pier overlooking the breakers. You could hear them crash all night. The house was approached by a pair of whitewashed gateposts and a long, long drive between charred potato fields and marshland. A stark infinity of plains. So much sky you could see the earth's curve at the edges. It felt like standing on the head of a pin.

Outside, the house looked like Dorothy's in Kansas, but inside, each room was a present that wrapped you up instead of being unwrapped. My bedroom was tiny, like the cabin of an ocean liner, and midnight blue. The elephantine white towels on brass towel racks were featherbeds to sink into.

I liked other people's houses. I liked their magical linen and towels that got changed invisibly. I liked the jellies they put in their baths and the sponges that looked like school food and got left in the sun to dry. The silent servants who seemed to move by remote control. "What you don't expect when you get old is that your servants get old, too," Mrs. Palafox warned.

But hers did everything so beautifully that you didn't notice that they did so little. The rougher work was executed by a fleet of boys from town, handpicked for their good looks but not trusted with the car. There was a little secretary whom Mrs. Palafox was mean to, with legs in white ankle socks and penny loafers in every shade of suede from magenta to mauve. (I had picked up, too, that usage of "little"; for Mrs. Palafox, as in French, a class distinction: charming little Mr. Crawford, the fishmonger who towered above her.)

It was a purer-than-convent life. I imagined the strait and narrow path not, as I once had, bordered by topiary and flanked at intervals by crumbling goddesses disporting themselves, but a more salt and windblown landscape: the gate no longer bearing pineapples but two plain whitewashed posts.

One walked without ranging. On sparkling days, the sky piled clouds high with the deftness of a lady's maid arranging hair. On overcast afternoons it was no boudoir scene, but vicious and mystifying as the water. We went swimming in the cold, foggy sea and could not distinguish its borders from the sky's. It was an idle but bare life, all brisk walks and swims and eighteenth-century memoirs. I told Mrs. Dawkins the night before what time I would want breakfast. I had succumbed to Mrs. Palafox's staple diet: black coffee, white yogurt. (The people I liked tended to stick to black and white, I noticed.) "Gotta have something to coat the stomach with," Mrs. Palafox proclaimed, after a pot of espresso had eaten its way through the lining. Mrs. Palafox woke at six, took a swim before breakfast, and spent the morning back in bed, talking transatlantic and screeching her memoirs at the secretary. She gave audiences, too—household petitions like a feudal castle. Mrs. Dawkins came to hear the menus. Maurice would come to argue about the borders. Sometimes I had my breakfast in her mammoth curtained bed. Then a lacquer tray was eased onto her knees at two, the curtains drawn, and outside—pale magic. A buildup of clouds. Salt-blanched long grasses. We met again over pure cold dinners of jellied soups, steamed vegetables chosen and arranged by color. Vichy water. A custard or apple tart. She read aloud to me in the Arabian Nights living room, or we watched the late-night gangster movie.

Mrs. Palafox didn't like girls and I didn't like the company of women, so we got along fine. "Of course everyone knows that in a scrape it is women who rise to the occasion: the cocotte with smallpox can't expect her beaux to break her deathside quarantine—men can't bear disease, only rivals. But at the best of times I find the company of men simpler and jollier," said Mrs. Palafox. And so did I. I didn't like people my age either. I didn't know how to play, and they weren't fooled by my fitful efforts at coziness. When I was little, I just beat them up, but then things got more complicated. It always seemed easier to be an old man's idea of a schoolgirl. It seemed easier to be an avenging angel or the hand of fate than a teenaged girl. It seemed more likely that I was somebody's idea of a joke. And yet to be scolded into a lady by Eustacius was no joke. Must I now be what I had always wanted to throw mudpies at the white linen of, must I now be Mem Sahib with the long pale fingernails?

Sometimes Mrs. Palafox had ladies to lunch, particularly trying ones, the kind Eustacius wouldn't have let eat off my great-grandmother's plates. They caterwauled in shop French, with their bathing suit straps tucked into their glistening bronze bosoms. They reminded me why I hated schoolgirl games: the bullying and the minutiae. But by late afternoon they had set out to cruise every china and linen store in town to pick quarrels with the shopgirls. Muffled curtsies of leftover awe for Mrs. Palafox, like dancing class. *"Bonjour, Madame,"* deep plié, and scurry out. The troublemakers were the ones who stayed for the weekend. Mrs. Dawkins packed a picnic basket full of magazines and Bain de Soleil, and Mrs. Palafox had me take them to the Beach Club, deeming her guests thus sufficiently entertained until dinnertime.

The Beach Club was a baked-brick and chlorine-scented citadel of Americanness. Nowhere else would discerning grown people with a staff of six at home queue up for a tray of hot dogs and cherry pie from the snack bar, or scuff on a pair of sandals to meet the dress requirements of the cafeteria and get canned spaghetti instead. Dowagers stripped of stateliness showing quivering slabs of thigh, skeletal fried women with breastbones like an abacus descending into folds of flowered sarong as grimly gay as paper rosettes on a chicken leg; scarlet lobsters come alive to squawk pleasantries to the plucked partridge at the next table.

There were sleek brown children wearing towels and

slicked-back hair. We eyed each other like strange dogs at the ends of leashes. They drank beer and had parties with fireworks and played chicken with their fathers' cars on the way home. They came straight from a well-bred Coca-Cola commercial.

You would think that I didn't like the Beach Club much, but I reveled in it. There are not enough hours left of my life to make up for those I didn't spend wrapped up in a wet, sandy towel, guzzling South Sides. I was torn between superiority over the pretty kids because I had Jem, and superiority over Jem because he would be so out of place. Mrs. Palafox would not set foot inside the club. She was too proud to be discussed at top volume by her old schoolmates, and too fastidious to enjoy sandy hot dogs and oily sunglasses. She dispatched her guests and sat on the lawn under an umbrella where her secretary read aloud to her and placed long distance calls.

I had gone with Maurice that morning in the old sedan to North Fork to pick up some lobsters for dinner—unless supervised, he brought back spindly consumptive ones. So many unexpected guests had turned up for the weekend: the Milanese architect had decided to bring his American wife, Marina, and her dog; and Olympe had decided to bring her husband and child and its nanny; and Mrs. Palafox was wondering where she was going to put everyone. I had already been moved to a trundle bed in the little cottage. The gaudies were in command; Mrs. Palafox even had to give them lunch, instead of packing them off with the picnic basket.

During lunch there was a telephone call for Mrs. Palafox, a furor of pleased squawks from her end of the line, everyone craning their ears to hear who it was. She came back an instant later. It was Jem. He was out in Montauk and had asked himself to dinner.

I went out to the dunes when lunch was over, to a place where you could stretch out and see, without being seen. The long grasses tickled and sang. From where I lay I could see Olympe's arrival, flanked by a fat Latin nanny hoisting an even fatter Latino baby, and a straggly string bean husband. I could see Olympe light on all the monsters of the party—ladies I wouldn't touch for a legacy—and kiss them all smackingly. The baby was passed around to be kissed, too: Tarzan Jubilee was his name. He was pawed and dismissed, and everyone came down to the beach for a swim. Aldo and Jean-Luc and the ladies in straw hats waded out to their waists in water and stood like water buffalo, slapping at the flies. From the long grasses every word carried across the water like a shot. I began to be sorry that I had not stood up and presented myself. Now I was stuck. The minuet of conversation: marvelous weather, marvelous water. Bow and turn. Isn't the house a dream? A little genteel shilly-shallying and go for the dirt, with that archness some people assume when they want to be disgusting.

"So sorry to kick that child out of her room—I feel such an intruder," began Olympe. She was chalk white, a voracious-looking girl with masses of red hair. She was an old girl friend of my father's.

"Oh, aren't you a goose to fret. Doncha know, kids just adore to scramble," said Mrs. Palafox.

"Somehow, I don't think Tarzan *ever* will," Olympe reflected.

"And, love, Le Petit Trianon is hardly roughing it," Aldo reminded her.

What an age since anyone one knew had seen Desmond. What was it he did now? Sold snuffboxes or something. He was recovering from the shock of marriage. No, he messed around with pictures. "And he's damned on the ball about it, too," said Mrs. Palafox smartly. "Not a bit airy-fairy."

"Does your *petite cousine* resemble Mama or Papa?" asked Olympe.

"I call her Creole," said Mrs. Palafox. "Long, high-stepping, white Negro sort of girl. With that cachet white things have—white peacocks, white asparagus, white Bengal tigers. After all, pet, it's an old Louisiana family; well, *old*— old just means sprung from French felons on the lam—but you can bet there's a touch of the tarbrush somewhere along the line. Don't look so appalled, you can see I've got the old darky blubberlips myself. Well, at least it means I can wiggle a hip. Nothing like rhythm for the circulation, and you live to be one hundred and two."

"Pretty eyes, that Jezebel has," Aldo remarked.

Mrs. Palafox would rather defend me than hear me praised. "Pretty, pale blue glass—I mean, you'd stoop to pick up a piece on the beach, but in a girl's head, not all there, wouldncha think? But not a bit of it. Her papa told me to keep her outa trouble, but really, the girl is *fulla* sense. Not one of these disco ducks at all. Good common horse sense—none of your *sensibility*. My secretary told me the other day I wasn't to yell at her. 'Mrs. Palafox, I am very sensitive.' I said, 'You're a prize fool, that's what you are. Use your noggin and I won't have to yell.' I like the girl not for the curve of her cheek or a head held like a flower, but for her guts."

Then the subject turned to the Chasms and Jem.

"I gathered Desmond's daughter is having a thing with young Chasm," said Olympe.

"Well, I don't think he's come out here for the pleasure of *my* company," Mrs. Palafox retorted.

There was a mild outcry. "So young! I always wonder what these girls will be like at forty," said Aldo sadly.

"I must say, Clo, if that's what you call keeping a girl outa trouble . . . ," Marina chided.

"What am I to do?" Mrs. Palafox demanded when prodded. "I'm in rather a bind, doncha see? I didn't invite Jemmy out here, but I've known him since he was an infant, and it would be a bit much to expect me to turn the boy away at the door. Anyway, I think Desmond's in a pet about nothing. Men always overreact so about their daughters' beaux. *I* think it's charming. Of course, nothing is going on. It's just a teenage dalliance."

"My God, coming from those two families, the kids must be crazy as coots. I wouldn't be surprised if it doesn't end in murder."

We sat in the conservatory drinking tea and rum in the late afternoon. She sat so upright in a sheet of purple on the edge of a black vinyl chair, stroking my leg and transfixing me with that slurred growl, issuing from a wet, slightly tremulous pout. I wanted to drink in her keen jeweled eyes, the slouchy, inhospitable projections of her figure: pelvis thrust forward, head back. An Asiatic monkey with Ivory Soap skin, and hair crimped in a chestnut wave. She wasn't a conversationalist, exactly; she talked without give or take. Catherine the Great's bed. A shoemaker in Lisbon. And slam—the Inquisition.

"I'm just thrilled to bits that you and Jemmy are all fixed up. I'm sure he's just bonkers about you. I always knew there was some spark behind those big bop-eyes of his."

"Oh, he isn't— We—we aren't—"

"Darling creature, I've seen it all before. I knew his father when Charlie was still head first over the Senora, and it's unmistakable—nothing like it on earth. And I think Jemmy such an attractive fellow. Now tell me, have you set a date?"

"Oh Lord, it's not even a romance, I tell you."

"My sweet, now I know your papa was not mad about the two of you monkeying around, but if it ends up at the altar, who cares about the jolts en route?"

"But I wouldn't even *want* to marry Jem—it's just a joke."

"Darling, you must be out of your mind. You can't go gal-

livanting around town with good looks and not all that much
cash forever. Now that you've got the boy, and one should be
saying bravo, you've got cold feet."

But that isn't it. At all. . . .

I did not want to see them after that. I wanted to stay in the
little cottage forever, floating in the shallow bath, dusting my
limbs with powder, making as immaculate a toilette as if I
were to be embalmed in it. I wanted to be put on ice, until
everyone I knew had died. The room was tranquil and white
as a beauty clinic. You get as close as living creatures come to
nothingness in a clinic. Laid out, in the still of a white room,
wrapped up to the chin in a white sheet, face petrified in a
white cold-cream mask. My father made Mummy send me,
when I ate so much chocolate he feared I would get spots. I
didn't, but I liked the salon for its demure and icy nothingness.

I didn't want to see Jem ever. His name had been a call of
the wild for so long, making a lapdog start and whine in its
after-dinner sleep. I had thought of him as an exile thinks of
home—of walks through forests and one's own books. But
now I didn't want to go home any more. The chatter of those
powdered sepulchers had soured the thought of him. And for
Mrs. Palafox's worldly complications I blamed Jem and not
the lady. He had spoiled my new paradise, and now we would
both be sent away. I could never have been a child who went
to barbecues, but now I wouldn't even know the price of top
sheets in Madrid.

They were having champagne on the terrace when I came
through the garden. The last light sharpening the traceries of
the balcony made the company look older than the local gods.
A squeal arose when I came up the steps. Eustacius would

have been shaking his head. Not much silver in the vocal register. They flimsies and parrots.

"*Quel spectacle!*"

"*Quelque chose, non?*"

"My dear," growled Mrs. Palafox, "doncha wish you were girl enough to put on a bit of lace and flowers in your hair and knock everyone dead!"

"Yes, that's style," Olympe agreed. "Wearing a little shift when everyone else is decked out in Saint-Laurent taffetas." (Marina just plain thought it was common.)

"No, that's youth. If I came to dinner in my shift and no makeup, you'd shriek."

I curled up next to my bossy savior.

"Did you swim lots, baby?"

"No," I lied. "Aldo beat me racing and I went off and sulked." Aldo, who had conscientiously not got his hair wet, winked.

It was Mrs. Palafox's affectation to serve champagne not in long-stemmed glasses but in short, square ones, wide as soup bowls. I didn't drink usually, but this evening I bolted down the measurement required to blur the edges of a conversation about plastic surgery, to dim the impression of Mrs. Palafox, restless beside me, muttering: "And where is our guest of honor?" Back to plastic surgery and fallen faces they all knew.

A slap of the screen door and Jem was before us, advancing with that tottery tiptoe walk.

I realized that I had never seen Jem in front of real people, and that, next to other men, it was not the wheezy old queen or the goose of a cuckold who looked odd, but this tall, tall child in dark glasses and stiff lips. He was carrying a mammoth striped bass wrapped in newspaper, for Mrs. Palafox. "The flowers in Montauk didn't look too savory," he explained. But I also hadn't realized what a little spic he was, and that his

black suit and his austere politeness to the other Europeans
were like letters from home.

Their grandfathers wore such summer suits, with a hat and
cane, and spoke as painstakingly—and miraculously I saw
Jem treated by Aldo, Olympe, Jean-Luc with the same fond
deference as if he were an old gentleman on a bench in the
park. It was a spell that missed Americans. He shook hands all
around, so that it was hours until he was before me. What did
I expect? I was expecting him to be proper before the grown-
ups, to play St. Aloysius who wouldn't let his mother kiss him.
I expected I would still feel cross, but we dropped together like
dominoes and stayed there so long, entangled in each other's
hair and shoulder blades, monsters of the deep together, that
we began to laugh. "Oh God, Jezebel," he whispered. I could
tell that he was near tears, but he stood me up properly,
straight as a soldier.

"Aren't you clever to have hunted us down!" said Mrs. Palafox, in a not altogether congratulatory voice, and we broke
up and reassembled. Jem went and sat with Olympe and I was
landed with her imbecile husband, who cast angry looks at
Jem for teasing Olympe in French, for making her laugh and
clutch him. I heard Jem, when asked to admire Tarzan, aired
one more time before bedtime, replying: "Yes, it's a dream and
a half. It looks like Chairman Mao. Now will you send it away
again, please?"

As Mrs. Palafox said, at least now everyone would stop
asking if the baby could really be Jean-Luc's. It had his witless
grin, more forgivable in the very young.

When dinner was announced Mrs. Palafox pried Jem and
the battered redhead apart.

"Jemmy, sweets, you take Coral in." That was the secretary.
Well, he nearly pushed the girl off her feet, from the terrace
to the glassed conservatory where we ate. Coral was the sort of
girl they don't make anymore. While demure and obliging

with Mrs. Palafox and me, she had this way of treating men like old shoes that was supposed to be seductive. So she addressed Jem in a snippy way, and imagined that she was making a conquest. Jem didn't understand. I heard flashes of their crossed signals bounce off the glass.

"Coralie—what a pretty name. Every cow in Normandy is named Coralie."

Coral, who did not like having such a low-class sounding name, hissed, "*Coral.* C–O–R–A–L."

"Oh, I see. Like the OK Corral. You see, foreigners are so obtuse about the enchanting things you Americans are called. We're stodgy about things like children—we tend to stick to the Bible."

"Coral *is* in the Bible. It's a semiprecious stone."

"Oh yes, now I know. It's that stuff that dies when it hits the surface of the water, like the Kraken. What are your brothers and sisters called?"

"I'm an only child."

"What a shame."

Dinner was as edgy as a barnyard where the fox has been prowling.

"Darling boy," Mrs. Palafox trumpeted down the table, "tell us where you've been and what you've been doing. Something frightfully romantic and troubled, I hope. Jemmy," she informed the table at large, "is one of our few remaining problem children. All these kids are so damned straight these days you've got to watch your language. It's too delightful to have one rebel left. What are you doing in America, sweets?"

"Oh, I'm just a wetback," said Jem. "New York's the only place where looking third world means royal treatment. Of course I always *felt* underprivileged, but now that I've become a Hispanic I practically get half fare on the subway."

"I must say," Marina said, "I do think reverse discrimination has gone too far. You can't call a mugger a mugger any more; suddenly he's culturally disadvantaged. The Democrats are to blame, I'm convinced: they don't want our votes any more—they're too busy sucking up to arsonists and drug addicts." She leaned over to me. "Of course, one can't say a word of this to Clo—she'll just rave about how expressive their long hands are, how soulful their gaze."

What are you going to be tonight, I wondered. Wonder child or malcontent or cold trifler? Perhaps a brand-new bag of tricks? But Jem was resisting categories. His tone was lacquered, alert, but unimpassioned. He made a mock of Mrs. Palafox playing him as a juvenile delinquent, but he wasn't going to be a perfect little gentleman either. No one knew quite what to make of him.

I stared at my plate. The lobster claws were leering at me, so I marooned them in the middle of the table. The lobster looked so human. It made me think how good Jem too would be to eat, and how nasty everyone else at the table would be. Mrs. Palafox too old, pecked-bare bones already. Coral and Marina too flabby. Jean-Luc or Aldo so sinewy they wouldn't please a goat, and as for Olympe, you'd get hepatitis or blood poisoning or something. But Jem would be a cannibal feast. Charcoal broiled, those light ribs would crunch like a quail's.

After dinner, Jem led me out in the garden where the tangled trees were made to dance and gyrate in the flames from torches stuck in the grass at intervals. We took the path that went underneath the pier to the beach.

"Is that what you've endured every night, those twittering dregs of society? And you, you calm blondness of a good infant, have learned too soon that being a teenager is such a consummate virtue that one needn't make conversation." Jem kicked sand at me. I kicked back.

"We've been alone in the house, Mrs. Palafox and I, until you all showed up. And I've thrived on it. I could spend my life out here, like this."

"About time I did show up—that's just what I feared. This Palafox you're so taken with, she's nothing but a society pimp, Scarlet, a scrawny vulture. Why do you think she's so fond of you?"

"She's doing Daddy a good turn."

"I'll say she is. They're hand in glove. She'll present you to her pinhead idea of the world, and she'll sell you to the highest homosexual bidder."

"Don't talk that cynical way, it doesn't suit you," I said, and then as an afterthought, "She sold me to you."

Jem was triumphant. "Then she's even cooler than I thought. She's right—you can do no better."

"Oh, shut up! I haven't even forgiven you yet. I haven't even started to sulk yet." And indeed, I began to walk quickly down the beach, kicking seaweed.

"Forgiven what?"

That I felt like a gasping fish out of water without him. That he had been in America and not told me. That he hadn't said good-bye. "It's too boring to explain."

"Please please please forgive me, angel. Don't be haughty, it would break my heart." It sounded as if he wanted to laugh. He had his hand in my hair, around my neck. I stopped dead like a stubborn horse and disengaged myself.

"Well, don't sulk," he said reasonably. "Hit me as hard as you can instead. I imagine you could knock me flat, if you liked."

But I kept on walking fast. I had to remind myself how I loathed that self-pity mingled with smugness that let him play poor little match girl and sugar daddy all at once. How dare he suggest I'd best remain under his protection when he'd run out on me, vanished in a jam, been in America for months and not called, not come to see me? He always pretended to be saving me from people who quite simply weren't fooled by him.

His snuff and his barber and his military tailor, his Jesuitry and his terrorism and his sonnets: it was like a hypochondriac's lineup of little pills before meals, like a magician at a children's party: he was all props and no soul.

We walked faster and faster along the cold gray sand until Jem gave in and decided to exchange information for forgiveness. I would never ask him where he had been, so he told me, in his hypnotically low tones.

"You see, I wanted to go far, far away from Oxford and everything rotting and stultified that I've known there and my father asked me to do something for him which I couldn't pass up. He's been asked to take part in a conference on international terrorism this November. Since terrorism is more and more tending to cross borders, the Western world wants to cook up some laws so that you haven't got some countries training and financing terrorists, some harboring them, some extraditing, and some electrocuting them. Daddy was asked to deliver a paper—which he should have been able to knock off in his sleep—but he's been all tied up, and he asked me to put together some materials with suitable conclusions."

"Did you come up with the goods?"

Jem seemed affronted by my doubt.

"Of course. I sat for six weeks in this bear pit of a research institute in Southern California, feeding off faded atrocities and getting more and more fed up with the crassness of all those attention seekers feigning causes. And I handed in an exquisite treatise with unacceptable conclusions: that an international paramilitary squad like the SAS should be established to shoot terrorists on the spot. No compromising with threats, whatever the price exacted. No aggrandizement of media coverage, of a highly publicized trial. And the press must be muzzled, since terrorism cannot function without publicity."

"But Jem, that sounds half-witted. Censorship of the press, government death squads? How are you going to get it past

Congress? Anyway, once you decide that criminals don't deserve to live, you're already thinking in a terrorist's terms."

"Liberal hogwash," murmured Jem.

"Well, what did you father say?"

"He junked it with thanks." Jem looked impassive. He knew he was right, but that no one else would ever think so. "Really, no one wants to change things. They just want to stand up and say the United States denounces Libya's unconscionable harboring of terrorists. They just want to lodge protests against one another."

Jem had got the sack. He was unfit for any assignment. It made my stomach dance with fear and embarrassment. I was trembling so badly that I could only try to tease him out of feeling like a misfit.

"So now you have some more suits made."

"Now I 'm taking you away with me."

"How can I trust you when you walked out on me?" I blurted out.

Jem sat down very suddenly on the wet sand, and plunked me down beside him. We sat awhile in silence.

"So what have *you* been doing with yourself?" he asked abruptly.

"I've been waiting for you."

He sprawled out on his back, brooding, combing the stars like a searchlight.

"I think you've got events confused," he said. "You walked out on me." He had just gone away for a day or two, he said, a little scouting around, told me to sit tight, and when he got back I was gone. "You couldn't wait. You couldn't trust me. You were too know-it-all. So now it emerges that you've been waiting for me after all—here, in the Hamptons. (How was I to guess that was what you were doing here?) Is it touching the way you save yourself for me? I don't find it touching. Frankly, I don't give a fuck. I've been dying for the loss of you. I don't care whether you've been playing whist with your granny or gun running in Central America; you haven't been with me, that's all I know. I suppose you've been walking with God. It has to be God, doesn't it—the archangel Raphael won't do. But why you think you can walk with God and also walk with me is beyond me.

"I've been in New York for days now—five days, in the St. James Hotel where tramps set themselves on fire in their sheets. I've been going back and forth past your house now and then—I won't give you the satisfaction of telling you how often. Not a light in the upstairs window. I felt so sad, I wondered how many of the sad-looking men going past were looking up to see if you were home, how many Spanish teachers who had never recovered from the blinding benediction of your gaze. And I prayed that someday you too would be that abject about some fellow who doesn't give a damn for you. (Remember I wasn't the one who said that I loved *you*.) And when you do, I hope you'll tell me the name of the saint for people who follow other people around and wait beneath their windows. Oh you know, I don't believe in God, but I've always believed in human goodness.

"Well, I finally got up the guts to telephone—I couldn't stand a Labor Day weekend of it—and Rastus told me the good news, that you were summering in Southampton. Glory be, Jezebel, you call that waiting for me?"

I didn't answer for a while. "Well, what now, Jem?"

"Now I'm taking you away with me."

"Where are we going?" I demanded, taking his hand in mine, like a child on a treat.

"I'm going to Chiapas, and I want you to come too."

But my face had dropped because the treat echoed Casimir's wanting to take me to Spain and suddenly sank to social currency of no greater value than "We must have lunch." And anyway, Jem's regularly announced departures for Mexico had

taken on by now the quality of a drunk's vows of abstinence,
so I only muttered, "Great."

"Talk about smoothness and sincerity—let's see that sincere, responsive smile of yours, the one I loathe. Shall I say it
again? I want you to leave *now*, right now, and come to live
in Chiapas with me. I've always wanted you to. What do you
expect me to say—that my life is in your hands (those sweet
dirty hands)? You know it already. I mean to take you away
from this chimpanzee's tea party of a life you've fallen into.
We'll try the mountains; enough of these mud flats."

"When are we leaving?"

"Tonight."

"Tonight is a little sudden." But I was beginning to believe
him.

"I'm giving you a wealth of choice. There's a freighter to
Vera Cruz tomorrow morning, or we can take the Desert
Creeper to San Antonio and board a three-day train to Guanajuato. I would almost take a plane to please you, but not
quite."

"Boat," I pronounced.

"You'll be sick as a dog all the way, but that's fine with me;
you've got rather puddingy this summer."

I could see the freighter waiting at the pier, fretting at its
anchor. The crew was getting footloose. Black poisonous
waters for a week, and you wake up in the Gulf.

"Are we going forever?" I asked.

"Oh yes . . . forever and a day. Why? Anything you need
in New York? Any unfinished business?"

"No."

"Are you sure?" He eyed me suspiciously. "Well, suit yourself."

"I'll miss Casimir," I admitted finally, realizing that I'd
never been alone with Jem, and that this was altogether his
own doing; that Casimir—that dummy, that wry gooseberry—

was always lodged between us to absorb the barbs of Jem's showing off, to sop the uncomfortable questions that were between us, to tell me the story of Jem that was dearer to me than the pinched flesh itself and the sallow blood of him.

But Jem, instead of gritting his teeth in jealousy, said, "So will I."

"Maybe he could come, too," I ventured.

"Casimir? Casimir will find his way to us. Don't you fret."

So Jem was going to live in the house in which Ofelia Bocanegra had been caged, which she had schemed like a wildcat to leave behind. Jem's bones weighted down with her jewels could now be sent back to bare rooms which screamed with her frustration. It was a revenge, and a reversion of dead people's escapes. He was catching his animal soul and dragging it back to its corral and now he would no longer be mad.

"Are they expecting you? Has the house been kept up?"

"Of course. Houses must be lived in. Nature has that loathing of walls and buildings that makes its tiniest minions conspire to undermine our preserves. Jorgito, the foreman, lives in the big house now. I telegraphed and wrote to say that we are coming."

"How many souls do you own?"

"The squatters', the tenants', and yours."

We were joined by Mrs. Palafox, Aldo, and Olympe, all tottering down the beach, arm in arm.

"What are you two doing?" Olympe demanded jealously.

"We are looking at the moon."

But there was nothing splendid about the moon that night. Its silver was not the silver of gleaming table manners, nor the silver of mines, surfacing in the discovered worlds. The moon was hysterical and fugitive, streaming out its alarm, reeling in another direction from the clouds it flooded, like the instant's panic of automobile headlights on a wild road.

Olympe plunged her arm through Jem's and bore him back to the house. The grown-ups were reclining on pillows on the terrace, their voices sedated to a hum; less insistent than the cicadas or the ocean. I was tackled by an insensate Jean-Luc, with unenthusiastic tugs from Aldo. It had got to the seamier end of the evening, when people could no longer articulate, but grappled and droned. Jean-Luc's hot little hands contrived to be everywhere at once, while he assured Aldo and me that I was his empress, that I made him feel like a virgin afresh. Then Jem was over us.

"Who is this dog?" he demanded. "You little bit of trash, don't you know how to behave? I want to see both your hands in your lap, and keep them there."

"Isn't Jemmy expansive tonight?" said Mrs. Palafox from across the terrace. Expansive? The gasping shortcomings of what language can express. Before the catch it screams to a halt, its exaggerations vapid, devalued currency.

Jem was a flame that all the supine moths tried to entice. He couldn't stay still but veered off at angles, swaying to the Calypso which reached the terrace in waves, rolling a hip with a tremor so tiny, so reflexive, to a song that went, "She only want you for Yankee Doodle Dollars." Then he turned raucous, teasing.

"C'mere, Jemmy," shrieked Olympe. "*Vas-y*."

Finally he flopped down beside her and she fondled him until Jem sunk his teeth into her hand. She squealed. "*Gosse! Tu es tellement méchant, toi!*" and he was off again. Eyes round as saucers—the sorcerer's apprentice letting loose satanic forces when his master is away. He veered over to where I sat on the arm of Mrs. Palafox's chair, and knelt by me fingering the chain around my wrist: a heavy gold offering from the monkey goddess. "You're all fettered. Who put this chain around you?" he asked.

"It's frightfully barbarian, doncha think—that butter yellow?" said Mrs. Palafox. "It was made in the twenties—the origins of costume jewelry that ladies could wear to lunch."

People were dropping off to bed now, or being dragged, like Olympe, who had been hoping for an assignation. Everyone except for Mrs. Palafox, Jem, and me.

"Beauty must go to bed," Mrs. Palafox announced. "Look at those heavy, heavy eyes just struggling to stay open. Well, I'm retiring, else tomorrow I'll be done in as a doornail," and she kissed us both smartly on both cheeks. "Jem, be good."

That was all I had to say. Could he be good when he knew every square inch of me, every raw nerve and tendon, danced under his scrutiny?

"Shall we go?" said Jem mildly.

"What about Mrs. Palafox? Why don't we wait until tomorrow and say a civilized good-bye?"

"She's sophisticated enough to make the worldly assumptions. We'll send her a telegram from the ship when it's too late."

"Tell her you finally popped the question and we're eloping!" I roared with laughter. Jem seemed such an unlikely seducer. "Oh Lord, Daddy will have to pursue us and call you out. Perhaps Eustacius would."

"Yes, that is how I've always imagined leaving this world—shot by a jealous cook."

So much had been forgiven already. My friendships were marked by how many boundaries I had crossed, and the more worldly the people and the more inviolable the peace surrounding them, the worse behavior they forgave. The best kind of trouble was trouble in Paradise.

I imagined being Mrs. Palafox the next morning breakfasting off an enamel tray in the ink-blue and silvery bedroom. It would feel as if one were a crocodile, to have skin as old as Mrs. Palafox's. Crocodiles lay in the mud, and the sun and the water simply slid off their backs. They were water repellent. My grandfather used to hunt crocodiles with a hatchet down to the Delta at Pilottown. He said, "Don't let their eyes above water or they'll up and fight." Breakfast in a lizard skin bedroom. Mrs. Palafox pretending to be a mountain the way one does with a tray on the knees: a mountain that would turn volcanic when Mrs. Dawkins came in with the news that I was gone. John, John, the gray goose is gone.

"Get your things," said Jem. He called up Paul's Taxi and we wandered down the drive to meet the cab. I took only a few dresses. I guess I didn't really believe we were going anywhere, and I wasn't lugging around that ironcast trunk for a joke, a joyride. Just a drive on the vaporous animal-vegetable night: wild animals on the prowl, all the crimes of tomorrow's papers in the making, and the only thing stirring around us was corn in the husk.

"God," Jem was exploding. "That little frog pawing you— I was astonished. And you with that petticoat virtually up to your waist. Can't you wear something a little more substantial? I know you don't get much of a clothes allowance, but really." And as he calmed down, "I will dress you in shot silk, petrol-green from head to toe," he pronounced. I was silent in a sudden fit of gloom at his proving to be just like other men when it came down to it.

The Chevrolet marked "Paul's" pulled up. There were two fat little colored girls in the back, with their scalps carved into the geometry of a million tiny braids. They were wearing party dresses and bare feet. Jem hopped in front.

"I'm famished for something sweet—that old rat only gave us raspberries," he remarked to the driver. "Where around here can we get something sugary before we go to the city? What's the name of that really cool Russian place where you get Peking Duck and hot fudge sundaes up at the counter?"

"That Silver's, but it close at six in the evening. Only place

round here you can eat at three a.m. is the Holiday Grill
Diner."

The girls giggled all the way down Montauk Highway to
the Holiday Grill. I wondered what two girls were doing riding
around in taxis at that hour; if the driver was their daddy, he
must have been more fun than mine or Professor Chasm. But
the girls must not have been all that different from me. They
were the only other people I had met who rode around in taxis
all dressed up and barefoot.

"Is that your husband?" they asked me, inclining their
heads toward the front seat.

"Yeah."

"How many children you got?"

"Five."

"Oh, you full of it."

A minute later it started up again.

"What you going to have for dinner at the Holiday?"

"I don't know yet."

"What's he going to have?"

"A milkshake, probably. What do you recommend?"

"Well, if I was you I'd have a bowl of chowder. And a club
sandwich, and a strawberry soda. That's what the Holiday does
best."

"Oh, you," the other girl complained, fanning herself.
"La-dee-da. When you ever been there?"

When we pulled up at the Holiday Grill and got out, the
little girls yelled after us, "Say hi to five!"

Jem let me stop at home, in the early morning, before even
Eustacius was awake. We sat in the kitchen in the half dark. I
wrote a bleak and brainwashed-sounding letter for Mummy
and Eustacius, who could not read anyway. I said that Jem
and I were going to live in Mexico. That I had been an awful

drag because I hadn't known what to do with myself, but that it all made sense now. That I was held in God's palm and that this was what I was meant to do. Then Jem set the paper doll on fire. *Carmen est très maigre.* And we left for the St. James Hotel, and climbed the stairs to a poison-green room with a soiled naked mattress and a basin in the corner oozing animal life. I crouched in the corner while Jem reduced all his clothing to a very small knot at the bottom of his briefcase, and we caught a taxi down to the pier in the early morning chill.

Ten

≋

I didn't enjoy the ride. It was not that there was anything in
New York or England I was sad to leave; places had only been
possible backdrops for Jem, people expedient. It was not so
much that I was frightened of being alone with him in the
wilderness, for I believed that what was between us would
never run out. But I could not believe that a boat so airless
and stinking, so contaminated a vessel, could take us anywhere I might want to go. How could there be a heaven, and
this rusty charger floating beneath it?

I pretended that I didn't exist, that I was cargo, something
as sleek and insensible as a refrigerator. Three times a day Jem
slapped me into consciousness, wheeled me sharply about the
deck, pinpointed where in the bland, sickening chart of the
Atlantic Ocean we now were. How could the Atlantic be this
choppy slop about us, not blue, but oily gray as a shark's belly?
I held my breath, as if passing a graveyard, until the daybreak
on which we reeled down the gangplank into too dazzling
white mist.

Jem dropped my suitcase on the dockside and began running, dancing, whirling in glee. "It's the Gulf!" he shrilled at the oily slap of waves against wood. "It's the Gulf of Mexico!"

At dawn, the seafront of Vera Cruz was a luminous pinkened white like a city of temples, all shining pavement. We ran down wide empty boulevards designed for parades and triumphal entries, and still cocooned in early morning fog. We battered ourselves against the salt wet wind. The only living things in sight were a few soldiers trumpeting a lonely reveille from the sea tower of the military academy. As the light of day turned harsher, more imperious, rending the fabric of the fog, the pinnacles of the seafront cinema palaces and ice-cream–pink marble hotels would begin to look moldy and bereft as fading carousel music. Soon the boulevards would be swarming with coconut-ice vendors and souvenir stands selling the Mexican version of the foot-long hot dog, with blind men flogging lottery tickets—they were always blind, like fortune—and the youth gangs that seaside towns spawn: those sassy, aging brats with teeth blackened from a diet of cotton candy and Vera Cruz rock. The boulevards would be reeking of cages of monkeys and parrots.

We watched Vera Cruz come to life as we waited for the seven o'clock train to Tuxtla Gutiérrez. The fish market was the first to open: stalls festooned with wreaths of pink, red, gold snappers snapping each other's tails, fishwives chattering and screaming. Jem bought a paper cone full of tiny gray shrimp which we crunched whole, except for the heads, while sitting on an iron fretwork bench in a black oleander park. Jem was wound up tight with that violent sense of occasion in which one can't flag for an instant or the treat will be wrecked. "Coffee!" he gasped. "Before we drop."

The cafés where coffee merchants celebrated and quarreled were still barricaded by chairs upside down or tables upturned on the sidewalk. We went instead to a cavernous sailor saloon. Swinging slatted doors opened onto a wooden floor crumpled with vestiges of long-ended debaucheries. A monkey-shrunk old man was sweeping away the trash of broken glass, and one black sailor was asleep at the counter.

"Are you happy?" Jem demanded over the rim of a cup of thick black coffee. It was so inappropriate a question for a creature honed to decorative torment that every time he asked it, I stared in resentment.

"Or would you rather be tucked up in a camp bed in the maid's room of the gardener's cottage?"

"Oh, I'd be back in the featherbed by now, and all the gaudies gone." I wasn't succumbing that easily.

"Except Queen Gaudy herself. Happy?" Jem repeated.

"Yes," I admitted finally, beaming. How could one not be happy as a clam in this saltwater city of silk and milk and rotten ambiguities?

It was a sort of way station between the sexes, Jem told me, reeling off stories of the bomberos during Carnival, where you were waited on by drag queens in homemade green satin ball gowns who begged to be taken home with you, violet breath tinged with garlic; of melancholy transsexuals with squashed-in faces like Pekingeses entwined with one teenaged sailor on a crying jag. And old creatures more dubious still with no eyebrows and too much rouge and archly nautical blazers and peaked caps who winked at you naughtily, or was it just a tic? Penny arcades crammed with androgynous waifs—every wreck a typology of Jem Chasm. He was transfixed by the memory. "Let's stay," I said.

"Come along." Jem shook himself free of it. "We'll find purer climes—a mountain convent."

The red dust and plush compartment of the Southern Pacific was like a glass vitrine caging in relics—a fragment of the Cross, the thighbone of Saint Eulalia. There was an ancient couple with gold teeth sitting opposite, who read comic books and sucked on boiled sweets in silence. Us. Who could say that conversation would not run dry, that lemon fizzes would not be the sweetness in our life, and three gold teeth between us?

Suddenly I fell into a chill and a trembling black coffee panic. I had to think of everyone brave who had landed in Vera Cruz before me—of Hernando Cortés and Professor Chasm—not to want to be back on board ship, sick in its careering belly. I wanted to roll these times back uphill to a day when shore was still before us, when all I had to concentrate on was not losing my lunch before I got to the side of the boat. I had to think of Jem telling me that I was a tough nut, that I was his baby doll, and to remember that he had organized my destiny for me—hitherto so troublesome and clouded. No more lolling about with glassy eyes. Mummy would be grateful. If I kept on taking after her side of the family, at least she wouldn't be there to see it.

"Perhaps the Pacific Ocean next week," Jem was saying.

"The Pacific? But we just got *out* of the Atlantic."

"We're going south toward the Isthmus, where the Atlantic Ocean is only an hour from the Pacific. Translucent breakers. Wouldn't you like that? Have you ever seen the Pacific Ocean?"

"No, and I never wanted to. Lousy hibiscus wreaths and undulating girls—not my dream."

"Mule," Jem teased. "None of your doughy incuriosity." And he plotted gaily the places we would go, eking out a staring-crazy itinerary that looped the loop every damned way but to Chiapas; how he would take me to the seedy Pacific resorts and by bus to Campeche, through the Yucatán, and out to the farthest point of Quintana Roo, to the Islas Mujeres.

"What about Cuba?" I demanded. "Isn't Havana sort of on the way, while we're at it?"

"I can't understand this reluctance to get your feet wet," Jem complained.

But it wasn't that I was averse to tramping, but that doubts of Jem suddenly set in, leaving me in a cold stupor. These spirited wanderings he was bent on made me fear for the life of this house near the border that had been waiting so long untended. Had Jem just dreamed it up? I had never doubted his stories until now; that Casimir was so famous a flouter of the truth seemed to make Jem, in compensation, the measure of veracity. I couldn't tell now whether Jem believed in this Mexican St. Helena he had chosen for himself, or whether I had called an unwelcome bluff.

"I just want to get to Chiapas," I told him.

"Hold your horses," Jem retorted, suddenly cold. "We've got all the time in the world."

"Where are we going now?"

"San Ildefonso de Nepomuceno. Don't look at me like a camel. What's it to you, anyway, whether we spend the night in Chiapas or Campeche? You can't tell the difference. You ought to learn to look and not just gape, Scarlet. Can you tell me, after having spent forty minutes gazing out the window, any of the principal crops of southern Mexico?"

I couldn't, so we both turned to stare out the window in silence, like the old couple opposite who had run out of sweets and through their comic books by now.

The train staggered and halted, and I pulled down the window all the way to be slapped into life once again. Already it promised to be a seething hot day, and through the cold breath of fog I could smell the stupefyingly candied, smoky smell that was Mexico. Bells were pealing from every mountainside chapel and city cathedral, and cocks were crowing. I could see one in the scrap of yard before us: a scarlet bronzed emperor posing each claw in the air, like a bird dog, before he stepped. Pigs and burros braying in imitation.

Animals imitate one another. But God knows where the donkey got his hacksaw cackle. A sound of sweeping, of radios playing, of avid conversation from the tumbled red bricks, half built, half ruined. What could they find to chatter about at that hour in the morning? Before they had read the papers or bathed, before they had had a cup of coffee. But even the yellow dogs were rearing up on hind legs to spring at one another, joyously re-engaging in their daily tangle, with stirred consciousness and renewed interest, and the sanction of custom. I felt the same pang of curiosity and envy I felt in driving through Spanish Harlem and looking from cab windows at ladies dressed to kill leaning out their windows to gossip, at men on the doorstep and children bathing in fire hydrant fountains and playing stickball in the street past midnight, and the radio all-night company. Why couldn't I lean out the window to see all my friends, and play in the street in the dark?

I stared hard out the window, pressuring Mexico to divulge its rhythms, its refrains. It was a country that lent itself to sugary abridgments and distortions, one of those landscapes we pass through in dreams, and in nightmares take the consequences for. Mexico cherished the broken exile, deposited him at the feet of the Virgin of Solitude. It cooed over the misfits and cut down the powerful. So many crosses on the highway. It was a country that banished gods, shot and enslaved emperors, a country of genocide and subterranean riches ravaged. In so bloody and perjured a place, ghosts will always smudge one's vision, like hordes of moths clinging to a lamp until its light is darkened. It was a country that could give Jem sanctuary if it chose. It seemed to have been waiting for us a long time.

And Jem, shuttered by dark glasses, hunched and pale, had certainly eaten the corn husks unfit for pigs.

The red earth and banana plants and mangrove swamps of jungle and desert and solid rock gave way to colonial honky-tonk as we entered San Ildefonso. It was a rich but sober city whose sixteenth-century palaces were turned municipal: the palaces of Justice, of Agriculture, of Culture, the Music Conservatory to which Jem's mother had fought to go instead of to the convent. And the palaces ran into thoroughfares of stinking, hustling, tawdry markets and dance halls. Jem was determined to buy me something at the marketplace, but we found nothing but pink plastic babies, which made him shy away schoolgirlishly. "Ugh!"

He was determined to drag me everywhere he had ever been in San Ildefonso on those well-bred hangdog mornings when his mother left him to wander. Jem skipped along parched pavement, flailing my suitcase and hunting down remembered sites in a changed scene. I trudged behind in a daze. The Nepomuceño Library in the old Bishop's Palace— a seventeenth-century bishop who spawned half a dozen nephews, all monsignors and dead by the age of thirteen. He wanted a solid front of supporters on Judgment Day.

The Biblioteca Nepomucensis was under restoration. Jem did not believe it. He was convinced that the city was turning it into the Ministry of Defense.

"Those military queers always dote on rococo."

We sneaked in through the back garden. White sheets from the stucco moldings down to the metal cages of little fat books, sleek and prosperous looking as high-polished riding boots. Chestnut and scarlet and gold. Workmen hung from the ceiling like sloths and sang in hot, blurred voices. We ran away. My head still sang against the white heat of the pavement. Jem charged ahead, for across the square from the Bishop's Palace was the Teatro del Luz, in whose Kleenex-box replica Jem had performed the *Rosenkavalier* for his mother.

It was a Last Days of Pompeii in pink and green marble: bronze lions sprawled on the steps, bronze impersonations of Comedy and Tragedy on the roof like burglars. A boy in an undershirt and red trousers with gold braid let us look around this act of faith—faith that you really were in a box in La Scala and not at a road show in a one-horse town.

Remarkable aqueducts, a Sanctuary of the Virgin of Guadelupe, the Provincial Archives: Jem's memory was relentless, fanatically retracing steps of which I did not know the pattern or the end. I willed him to stop, to look at me, to hold my hand. I thought about dropping dead and would he notice I wasn't following? Impatience struck a compromise with exhaustion and Jem said, "I think we'll skip the Pantheon of Mummies, if you don't mind. A little too close to home. We'll go to the State Museum instead."

"Sweets," I told him, "it may be a one-horse town—well, this horse is just about ready for the glue factory." I would have feigned an epileptic fit by then to get him to pay attention to me.

Jem spun into solicitude on the instant, piling me into a taxi to the park, sitting me on his trenchcoat in the grass with a hot kaleidoscope of scandal magazines arranged around me. *Los amores tórridos de JFK. Marilyn Monroe—una estrella o una galaxía?*

We brooded sweetly in the dank shade of the Bosque Cuauhatémoc, a black Luxembourg crammed with statues and bandstands, until Jem got restless. "This town is charmless," he complained. "I'm too old for pomp and kitsch. Why don't we simply take a bus to one of the hill towns? I feel like something lofty and demure."

He spread out the map of Mexico on the grass, a map frayed and flayed by long serpentines inked across the south in green. He had come to life again at the thought of change, from lolling disconsolate to gesticulating, jabbing pinpoints in the map. Motion was the life-lengthening charm. If you felt low in one city, you simply rushed to the next.

"We are here, in the nineteenth latitude," he explained.

"The easternmost point on the chain of colonial silver-mine towns, each with a gargantuan basilica and a university built by the grateful rich of the Third Empire—more universities than Ohio, this province has. We should go to them all, all these glowing, bulbous cities, to Dolores and San Sebastian, to Magdalena and Catahualpo. There's a seventeenth-century hill station overlooking Magdalena—its weak sister, you might say. A conventual *jeune fille* of a sister where Magdalena's rich shopkeepers in the nineteenth century built small summer houses to look like little Parthenons. There's a hotel there, in an old hacienda called La Ventosa—that's Mex for Wuthering Heights. I'll take you there when we're fed up tramping."

I could see Chiapas on the map, and this freshly inked galaxy of stars led brazenly away. We were going nowhere but to hell in a handcart.

"We can catch a bus for Dolores from the Plaza del Luz," Jem was saying.

"Can I go to church first?"

"But why? Mexican churches are all alike inside," Jem protested.

"I want to pray."

I had not thanked anybody yet for getting me off that ship. Jem walked me to the Basilica. He was mollified by its eccentricity, its spires all swirling baked clay, red honeycomb—the flying inspiration of an architect who had seen mezzotints of the French Gothic cathedrals and crossbred their spikes with Russian onion domes. He let me go inside, while he waited on the steps.

Inside, it was a museum of dusty vitrines and stuffed exhibits, a taxidermist's delight. One fat Cristo Rey in red velvet boxing shorts like the Young Contender confronted a staggering Christ bent double under the cross, whose sharp teeth and glass eyes expressed a deranged anguish. His yellow satin robes were weighted down with an army of tiny silver arms and legs and flaming hearts.

Walls of tin paintings by grateful petitioners. Tin tablets of railway trains running off their tracks into gorges, of steamers with two funnels sinking. The artist on his knees in a dormitory, and the Madonna descending on a pink cloud to the iron bedstead. The Virgin to whom you pray when hope is long gone. Purify me, Mother of God of Hosts. Electrify me with your blue. Petrify me with your pink cloud. Carve me open with the lightning bolts that glide between. Keep me brightly lit and constellated as your image.

I had begun to loathe the waxen dolls for their puffy arrogance that seemed to say that they would never be banished or superseded: *they* were too cute. "Buddy, you never know what's in store," I wanted to tell that simpering St. Michael. "I always used to slap my ex-best dolls and pull their hair out before I got bored."

There were only two other people in the church: an old man who stood still, arms straight out at either side with the palms upward, chanting dolorously at the top of his lungs, and a woman in black lace who crawled on her knees from entrance to altar, knocking her forehead against the floor and kissing it. I was jealous of their certainty. Was their God mine? If so, he must love them better than me. They had doled out their wages to buy stuffed saints like Goldilocks, the latest in saintly fashion, and they continued weekly to support those dolls' voracious habits. They splurged on St. Michael's booties the way I splurged on taxis. It was a necessary luxury, and you loved your own because it was yours.

I lit three candles before the Virgin of Miracles, and asked, "O Mother, let it be all right," but I did not know what was wrong. And then I went out into the light of day and the steps full of pigeons.

Jem had bought me an ear of corn doused in lemon and chile and rewrapped in its husk from an old woman who sat roasting corncobs over the coals of a fire at the street corner. He was pink with excitement at being able to buy such a feast on the street. He had found the right bus stop and was being quashingly efficient now. I felt game for another fight.

We boarded a crowded bus to San Saturnino that was red and yellow spangled and called the Inferno Azul. And Blue Hell went rocking and reeling along mountain passes and all I could think about was the tin paintings of buses going off the edge of precipices. I leaned against the two women I was packed between and tried to look at the view. A landscape like the landscapes knights rode past searching for the Holy Grail, a landscape of pink-gray peaks, turrets of rock in which Siennese painters would have placed a St. Jerome. Pink lagoons surrounded by black volcanoes; pointed cypresses. Only the high Sierras were blue; every other pigment the landscape had plucked for itself—every Pompeiian red, burnt sienna, every poison- and ice-green, down to hell's own black-green, every alabaster and ocher. Even the sky was a decadent lavender. Even blue hell was red.

We crossed a long concrete bridge over a dried-up inland sea. Dead sea things were impaled in its dry, dry sand. Parched but gracious roads streamed away from the dead sea with wild promises, but leading into desert.

We were told to change for the bus to Dolores on the far side of the dead sea down by the café on the mud flats.

"About time," said Jem. "I thought those fat old ladies were going to steal you. You certainly have a curious penchant for old ladies. One simply doesn't cuddle with strangers in this country."

"They didn't mind."

"They don't."

The café on the shore of the dead sea was a poured concrete block painted aquamarine, as if in compensation for the unwateriness of its sleeping partner. Pink letters said "La Brisa de la Palma."

"The slap of the hand," I repeated in delight.

"The palm breeze," Jem corrected.

Inside, the proprietor was celebrating his daughter's first communion. Around a long banquet table all his relatives shouted and sang and feasted on crabmeat wrapped in tortillas and dunked in salsa verde. We stood awkwardly in the doorway, uncertain whether to go or stay. But the father stood his little girl on a table for us to admire: a sugary poppet in floor-length white lace which got dunked in the bowls of green chile sauce. The guests cheered and Jem complimented her parents in his stiff Anglo-Castilian lisp. I got the impression, as I had before, that he could not speak much Spanish, and it was the sort of occasion that brought out all the graceless, self-conscious English in him. He finally presented the child with a wooden pearl-studded cross from his toilet case. Her parents sent for a couple of bottles of local champagne and asked us to sit down with them. But Jem turned shy suddenly, and after I had sat down said we mustn't intrude on such a holy day. He took a bottle of Tehuacán water out on the steps by the shore instead, and I followed.

Outside the Brisa was stationed a pickup truck full of children in party frocks and patent-leather pumps. A fat boy in knickerbockers was engaged in lighting a firecracker under the tail of a caramel-colored spaniel. He looked like one of the church saints.

"That is the kind of dog the Aztecs used to eat. Come to think of it, that is the kind of boy they used to eat, too," said Jem.

He was waiting at a pained distance from me. He had sunk into misery, wondering whether his mother's cross had been a disproportionate present, too bent on knowing Mexico better than God Almighty to ask whether I thought so too, yet wanting it back desperately. He bit his fist and would not talk. Selling the Savior for a bottle of Mexican champagne, for camaraderie of the sort that always made him frightened and fastidious. He could never bear standing close enough to people to smell them. He could never bear accepting kindness, and the subsequent familiarities it induced.

"I suppose they think it's trash because it's wooden and not gold plate," he said with a sudden viciousness that took me aback. "Do you suppose if I offered them some money or something they would give it back to me?"

"Leave it. Let it go," I said.

Jem started biting his nails and knuckles, grimacing and swearing under his breath.

"Take my mother's," I told him finally, delving into my suitcase for that pinkened ivory cross that had come along with the marbles. "It belonged to the Negro cook my great-great-uncle married. He brought it back for her from the West Indies where she came from."

It didn't. It came from some smart antique store, but Jem was a sucker for uncouth exotics. He brightened, although he objected. "It would look prettier against black skin. Why did you get his things? Hadn't they any children?"

"They were never legally married, and when he died the Dableverts grabbed the entire estate and fobbed off the mulatto children with an annuity."

Jem was revived into a disquisition on Negro slave laws. That quality of coming to life out of a sullen coma was Mexican, that catapult into animation I had watched from the train window that morning in a hundred backyards. They slept on broken rubble and glass, these people, they ate fried mud and dust in old candy wrappers, but they rose glowing, the young like ripe fruit bursting out of its tattered husks, and in old age stately and straight-backed, the men like scarecrows, in straw hats and pantaloons their stick legs didn't fill, the ladies white-paper–skinned or dried-apricot–faced, in three petticoats, two skirts, an apron, and a shawl. Beggarly dignitaries who each seemed possessed of one obscure distinction, village idiots who were pointed out to one to say, I dined once with Diderot, I killed off Rasputin when he would not die. Warmonger faces. Glinting arrowhead eyes. These old kept their secrets: savage, down-swooping machete-blade mouths did not senseless spill the beans, toothless suck on the same stories. No maudlin, arms-akimbo drunk grandfathers goosing lampposts.

When the bus that pulled up was called El Nuevo Mundo we felt like conquerors. We had a seat to ourselves and in this small cage of space, with our elbows and ribs economically interlocked, Jem, lulled by the discomfort and airlessness, began to talk of his earliest travels. It was a rare and frightening treat.

"Mama was a breakneck traveler," he said. The name made us both shy; Jem played with his new cross until he could speak with the suavity of an evangelist. "Once arrived, she immured herself in the hotel suite, so that it seemed as if she would only leave feet first. You would think that one hotel bed was as good as another, but so soon she would get bored. And then she insisted on racing from city to city across continents. But neither of us drove, and neither of us would fly, so it was a real journey of the Magi—a succession of trains, taxis, steamers. Well, even the back of a camel is comfortable compared with those red velvet and horsehair pallets people sat on in the Spanish émigré drawing rooms she grew up in. She didn't approve of comfort; it was like fat. She only liked her own way, and that was the most difficult one."

Jem rambled, with a rare sweetness and tolerance, but while he talked I boiled, fed up in retrospect with the incompetence of Jem's carrying on at the dead sea café, chewing on the suspicion that he didn't know what he was doing, that he didn't want to be here.

"Where are we going, Jem?" I was angling for a brawl, and when Jem spun out an itinerary that zigzagged all across the subcontinent, in no particular order, I blew my top.

"Why don't we just hop a jet to Daytona Beach and forget about it?"

Jem suggested that I learn some of the eighteenth-century virtues, like equability and good temper.

"Trade me in," I urged him. "I think you can probably find yourself another babydoll reeking with equability on a high-chair at any of these roadside stands."

Jem had subsided into meekness. "I've got no desire in the least to ditch you. You are the one who is getting fractious. I simply want you to let me have my head until we get used to this country. You must remember, I haven't been back in years. Places change; you want to beat the bushes to raise a few recollections, catch the scent of the new."

But it wasn't the delay that vexed me. It was that we were going nowhere at such a great rate and, little as I wanted to, I couldn't help questioning Jem's stories. Was there a house in Chiapas? Maybe there had been one, but surely long ago sold. No dour Jorgito in white pantaloons to welcome us, no bridal bed draped in white lace curtains daily aired over the years. Houses didn't stay waiting for seventeen-year-old boys to grow up and come see them. Who was this Jem? And once doubt and suspicion set in, there was no saving us. For Jem had been my refuge. If he was a liar, what truths could buoy us? Jem glanced at me sideways, chin on his chest, knees drawn up to his chin, trying to gauge what I was thinking, looking his most winsome, but the winsomeness was a tic of pain, of pleading. He was frightened by the silence, and I was too sunk in doubt to calm him. The taut intimacy between us had suddenly dis-solved, as if it had never been, and his stilted courtesies only underlined this recognition that we didn't know each other, that perhaps there was nothing between us but a shared hollowness and dread.

I dreamed you and I woke up, I told Jem in my head. Now, dream, go away. Jem was smiling at nothing and his smile became more pained and lopsided. A friend of my grandfather's had ended up like that: a bad-tempered old man whose face was paralyzed by a stroke into one crooked grin of idiot indulgence. My mother took me to his house when I was little. I remember smiling back, determined to do what was expected, until I realized his smile was stuck, and I started to cry. I stared at Jem and didn't cry, but I didn't feel like smiling either.

It was a long ride and there was nothing to say. We could no more gossip about Casimir, quarrel about our fathers or Mrs. Palafox than if we were the sole survivors of a tidal wave that had drowned them all, because it was Jem and I who had drowned them. The expanse of our new world was one razed to a surface too raw and scarred to look at, one unrecognizably, unbearably disfigured.

"You don't want to go to Chiapas. You don't want to live here. Why don't we pack it in? Go back to England?" But Jem, terribly, wouldn't answer.

We were hurtling along a plain scattered with starving whitened shrubs. Hell only knew what direction—the sun was dead overhead. Jem tried to push open a closed window, but the catch was stiff and he clumsied by dread and obduracy.

I softened. "I don't care—I wouldn't care—whether we were going any place at all, if only I were sure of you," I brought out at last. But now Jem drew himself up like a king cobra, flaming into a sudden bitter anger.

"Sure of me? *You* need to be sure, you two-bit slut, you know-nothing? What do you mean by that? Sure that I will amount to something? Is that it?" He was on the edge of some hysterical denunciation, but I could only stare in astonishment.

"No, that's not what I meant at all."

"Well, I won't," he snapped, accusingly. "I won't amount to anything. What's it to you? What have you got to offer?"

"That's not what I meant. I only wanted to know . . . to be sure . . . that there was something between us. . . ."

It was false and mawkish, this appeal, and Jem rightly would not answer. He was staring blindly out the window, his face averted. He was on the edge of tears, tears of humiliation and self-pity. It was true he didn't want to go on, but there was no going back, either. Jem who had expected so much of himself, was now of those who came furthest behind. He had done not differently from anyone else his age, but less and worse. He couldn't now try to join the chase but only sink himself out of sight. But where was he to go? Disappearing wasn't so easy after all, not if you took someone along with you full of insistence and reproachful questions. And all I wanted was to go away. Anything but tears, because Jem's tears would be like a drowning man's arms about my neck. To disengage myself from this situation would mean breaking each brittle finger. I couldn't now pretend I had come to watch the shipwreck as men used to watch hangings at Tyburn; I couldn't now say, "Poor boy, what a waste," as his parents' friends did.

"Get out," said Jem, "get out of it now. I don't want you here." He seemed to mean it, and I couldn't blame him. He was very white and his eyes had gone out without so much as a death rattle. He turned his back to me. Crammed together as we were on the little plastic seat, complete estrangement was out of the question. The bony hip and shoulder turned toward me prodded my flesh painfully, prodded me into a transfer of wrongs. I thought very long and hard about all the bad things he had done to me, until I decided that I would go back to New York.

I held several conversations in my head with Jem—a funny one, a heartbreaking one, and an impressive one in which I told him I was going back because it was a situation which only enlightened affection would have made bearable. I took a tremendous fancy to that phrase, and repeated it to him again in a number of modes. But when I remembered that the real Jem would only scoff, I felt so wronged by him that when the bus next halted I tumbled down the aisle and into the road. Jem didn't stir.

I had climbed out into a red heaven of jacaranda trees and tumbledown red-tiled huts, from which came running on staggered legs brindled mongrels with yellow eyes. Scabrous roosters eyed me. Under the scorching sun a child in a furry snowsuit was sitting in a ditch. I started walking south, along fields plowed by teams of oxen plum-colored like water buffalo. I wondered where I would sleep that night and the next, and wished I had thought to take my suitcase, and wondered would Jem throw it away in anger. I could sleep under a maguey. Cramped and spiny, but dry. I thought if only I had brought the flick knife I had bought on 42nd Street and Broadway I could be a bandit, but that, as it was, I couldn't even steal a chicken, unless I intended to swallow it raw. How flatfooted it would be to get sent home, C.O.D. But where was home and was all forgiven? I would never go home.

I had fallen into a sleepwalk, a sedate jog, when suddenly I woke up, heartsick with missing not my mother, not my father, not Eustacius, not Jem, but the blubbery boy who worked behind the counter of a kebab shop which Casimir patronized in Charlotte Street. It was open all night, and Casimir took me there often that first summer in London, whenever he came up for air between A-Levels. Casimir and the proprietor's son had a rather queasy intimacy based on some joke I didn't know.

"Hullo, sweetheart," Casimir would say.

"Hullo, babes." The boy grinned. "What will you have, honeybunch?"

I missed the Acropolis. I missed its red cracked vinyl stools, its Formica, its frescoes of Ancient Greece. Its menu had particularly provocative descriptions of each item: "Moussaka: A Greek favorite and our specialty. Succulent minced baby lamb in a sizzling bed of aubergine, topped by a luscious bechamel custard."

"Sizzling bed—sounds just like home," Casimir observed. And then mysteriously, whether one chose baked Alaska or beef stroganoff or a pink lady, they were—just that minute— out of it. In fact, they were out of everything but shish kebab and taramosalata. When we went there with Jem the following year, he took pleasure in ordering everything on the menu in turn. "Oh. Chicken Kiev was just what I was craving. No? How sad. Well, then I'll have crêpes suzette," until the waiter was shamed into admitting the diminished state of their deep-freeze that night. Casimir was offended by Jem's cruelty to his darling. He swiveled his stool around and pretended to be a stranger behind his newspaper.

Both boys always stuffed their pockets with books and newspapers, perhaps so they could play strangers more easily. They read going up in elevators, sitting in traffic jams, or whenever one displeased them. Mostly they read maps and Baedekers and travel accounts.

English travelers were an odd and impassioned breed, I thought. Not the bilious, self-aggrandizing exile who found he could live cheaper in Italy, but the flamboyant chameleons—mostly sickly, mostly homosexual; both good reasons to look for a constantly shifting landscape. There were the parasites of change who flung themselves into the costume and the local color, the element of pantomime and unreal dangers. There were the adventurers, in every shade of scurrilousness from Richard Burton's high-spirited villainies to criminal imposture, double agents without missions. And there were the travelers with a cause; the martyrs, the missionaries, the discoverers—the Doughtys, who scorned their chosen land at every staggering step of the pilgrimage, the Darwins, who scorned the native. The fanatical, the sanctimonious. There were those who sentimentalized the Bedouin, those who slept with them, those who loathed them living but liked their ruins or their creed.

Casimir was a Byron without a cause, but Jem was a Doughty, that biblical, classical, Old English scholar who prided himself on his cramped verse and considered his maniacally vivid and impassioned *Arabia Deserta* of interest only for its almost parenthetical description of Petra.

But then Jem, who liked nothing better than to overturn one's every smug theory to prove that life won't stay put, when I would have labeled him a desert father, had cried frivolously, "I travel because I want change, change, change! I want to be grabbed by the scruff of the neck and hoisted out of my sad, stiff self."

(But in fact it was Casimir who chased change across Asia in the back of black marketeers' pickup trucks, while Jem had strayed no farther than the Côte Basque, and for change sat at the counter of the Acropolis in Soho, reading *An Account of Two Voyages to Australis Novis and Back in HMS the Safe Return*, until Casimir had finished sulking.)

I was walking toward Dolores. It was under Jem's training that I even knew which way Dolores was, and which towns came in between. Under Jem I had learned to memorize the masses of provinces, veined with highways and rivers and mines, that make up a country, and the natural borders of Sierra Madre and Sierra Nevada, Rio Grande, that carved it up again. I even knew that the next town I came to would be

San Sepulcro, in the main square of which was Jem, sitting on my suitcase, reading Augustine through dark glasses. I could have eaten Jem alive with kisses, I was missing him so badly, but I wouldn't have said so for all the world. A horde of children were plucking at his sleeves, each with a scalp shaved bald from lice. I had never seen so many bald children in my life. Jem had been teaching them to play marbles the English way, and they clamored still to be played with, but he ignored them now. He hated children—an envious nihilism toward anything soft and petted. But he could, half-didactic, half-malign, supervise the play of little things.

"I've won seventeen pesos. Do you think that might be enough to support your nasty habits the next time you run away?"

He handed the change to me. He stood up now, hoisting the suitcase onto his shoulder. "And here is your case—you might take it, next time." Then he swung his arm around as if pitching a curve ball, but instead hit me with the suitcase, hard, across the cheekbone, so hard that I was knocked off balance and into the mass of children.

"Don't you *ever* pull that kind of spoiled brat tantrum on me again," he said.

"How dare you hit me in front of strangers, you suppository, you pig-stop, you eunuch . . ."

"Well, *strangers* . . ." said Jem, in soft depreciation.

"Well, are they friends of yours, those bald children? I thought you had given up cheating your friends."

"Have a Coca," said Jem. *"Es la refresca la más refresca."*

He gave the children too much money and took me by the arm over to the nearest sidewalk café. We sat down under the awning at a wooden table covered in a starched lavender cloth. I ordered hot chocolate and a club sandwich. The only other customer was the manager of the Santa Fe himself, a man in a black and white silk houndstooth suit, wasp waisted and shoulders grossly padded, who was doing his books at a far table.

The main square of San Sepulcro at teatime was a vision of the past sweetly sinister. At the center of the *zócalo* was the castiron bandstand, now painted silver, which the Empress Carlota gave to every town in Mexico; it still had about it a scent of music box Meyerbeer, of decaying full-length Winterhalters in the heat. Around the bandstand, plantain trees leant a shivering green awning over the fretwork benches: a married man meeting his teenaged girl friend—the gentleman jaundiced and pressing, the girl pale and triste; a bench packed with round red Indian ladies eating ice cream and giggling, four generations of them. An organ-grinder was playing all those sweet sad songs that make one miss something never known.

The club sandwich was the first thing I had eaten all day, and it disappeared in a gulp, crusts and all, leaving nothing for the hopalong parish dogs to carry away. I had been a fastidious eater before, rapacious only in swan dives of the fork, tiny bites, but fastidiousness deserts you pretty fast.

Jem started drawing on the tablecloth: a golliwog in houndstooth, and, remembering the pink and green opera house in San Ildefonso, a Mexican Octavian in breeches singing to a boxful of Indian ladies with ice-cream cones. It was a gesture of reconciliation.

"I think you are more Mexican than you'll admit," I said finally. "Don't they all knock their girls about?"

He ignored the last part. "I should say I'm not. Mexicans are gracious through and through. If it had been up to me, I should have put Maximilian in a cage. They actually put up with the seven thousand nightingales and bandstands Carlota unleashed upon them. Not to mention her goddamned receptions. 'Madame and good sister,' she wrote the Empress Eugénie, 'my Mondays are really most successful.' Her Mondays be damned. Monkeys in party dresses. And yet, even now, the Mexicans are charming about those two: a tragic couple. A tragic fraud."

"But they put him up against a wall and shot him."

"Exactly. What could be more civilized? He could have landed at the bottom of a mineshaft like the Romanovs. Even the death notice was charming. Occupation: Emperor. Cause of death: Heart failure. How could one expect such grace out of that mélange of two hundred Indian tribes bred with Frenchmen, Spaniards, Negro slaves, Chinamen, Moors. . . ."

"Chinamen?" I echoed.

"There was a route between the port of Acapulco and the Orient. Unimaginable riches went both ways. If we ever stop in that godforsaken ditch Salamanca, you will see that the cathedral is domed in jewels from Macao. All the sequins on saints' dresses are Chinese cash. And roadside stands scattered across the south will be called Café Macao, El Shanghai. Because, you see, in the eighteen fifties when the railroads were built, no Mexican would work on them, so they imported coolies."

I was cold and hungry still. I felt as if I would always be cold and hungry and tired. But I didn't care any more. The circles under Jem's eyes, too, looked graven. It seemed as if just while we had been sitting at the Santa Fe they had deepened from lavender to a golden purple.

"Where are we going, Jem? Let's hit the road."

Jem would not meet my eyes. "Do you want to go home?" he asked.

"No, Jem, I want to be with you. That is all I want."

If I loved him—and he was all I had ever loved—this jangling skeleton with pug dog eyes twitching between obstinacy and a craving for support; if I loved him, what did it matter where we went? I would rather be with him at the bottom of the sea than in heaven without.

A Cadillac with fins pulled up. Jem left some money on the table and pulled me into the backseat.

"Senor Cassim?" the driver asked.

"You called for a taxi—you would have left without knowing where I was?" I was outraged.

"Yes, I was going cruising," he said, "for you."

"Where are we going?"

"Where do you want to go?"

"Three more towns and then the best hotel south of Magdalena." I wanted to wake up in my own bed, but it was too far away even to think of.

Eleven

It seemed like days and days of it. Dogged, dusty days, raising ghosts of white dust, red dirt, black soot along the main streets of ghost towns. Yellow pariah dogs turned their backs to us and hobbled away as we approached. Squat Indians pressed their noses flat, expressionless, against the windows of our taxis. I had come to loathe their bronzed pug faces of a blankness that could express anything malign. The sickly smoky smell that rose from the dirt made me gag. Only that morning I had inhaled it as deeply as my lungs could bear.

The parks and cathedrals and municipal palaces of the larger towns were already muddled in my mind, already imbued with the golden glaze of time. Drained, bop-eyed with weariness, had we only that morning come down the gangplank? Could there be an end to such a day? Our driven pilgrimage across scorched concrete and white powdery quarries could end in no holy spot.

And how and why did it come about that Jem and I were in bed? It was late afternoon, the heat kept out by the whirling wooden fan upon the ceiling, and the sunlight kept out by the slatted wooden shutters that cast reflections of underwater currents across the walls. It was as if I had caught a mermaid with shivery tropical scales about to gray, like a landed fish's.

How long I had wanted him wrapped around me, and had trusted to his inviolable chastity. How long I had wanted him to swear all love's promises. To surrender. Or would it, could it happen, be one more dancing lesson with gritted teeth, in which he commanded me to melt? I guess I hadn't wanted to find out after all. But it was Jem who shut the bedroom door and leaning against it, pulled me to him with a sigh, who wriggled out of his clothes and into my arms, who fell on me and pressed his way into my heart like a fish through the water, like a dolphin, all the while saying into my hair, "Will you be very brave and bear it, Jezebel, will you give it a try?"

I loved him until I couldn't love him any more lest I burst. I pretended to be asleep afterwards so as not to embarrass him while he took me in from head to toe, learning by heart my ankle, the curve of my hip, my breast and neck. The agonizing sweetness with which he touched the bruise on my cheek where he had hit me in San Sepulcro. When I stirred, Jem climbed out of bed and went over to the basin in the corner. I watched him run his head under the faucet and wished I could die.

I felt at that moment that we could sleep together for a century in the high starched bed which was waiting for us in Chiapas, we could get old and fat together on the fretwork veranda in the jungle and the volcanic mountains; one day he might call me his darling and his own, and even so I would never feel less far apart from him. He didn't know how to surrender, nor I how to claim him.

I watched the ritual of his dressing, as it took him farther and farther away. Unknotting a white shirt from the bundle of clothes at the bottom of his briefcase, climbing into a pair of blue jeans, cinching in the crocodile skin belt, sliding into basketball sneakers with broken laces. I was transfixed by urgent details. How Jem filled his clothes no more than a clotheshanger might. The blue sheen to his wet hair, the greenish circles under his eyes. I watched him take a slug of mescal from the half-pint bottle he had bought in Magdalena, and slide the bottle into his trousers, snug in the shelf of his hipbone.

"Come on," he said, "I'm starving. Let's go scavenge." I wanted to cry, but instead I was out of bed and dressed by the time Jem had parted his hair. Before he put on a black silk blazer, he drew a pistol from his briefcase and slipped it into the inside pocket.

"What's that?"

"It's a Luger."

"Who needs it? We're only going to the goddamned market." We had a slight scuffle over the gun, but he let me take it away from him and put it under his pillow.

"Sweet dreams," I said sourly. But I was jealous; I had always wanted a gun too. I wanted more than the moon for it to be said of me, "She's a crack shot; she can hit a rattlesnake between the eyes a hundred feet away."

We ran downstairs and across the cobblestones of the courtyard toward the main square.

"Where did you get it—in California? Stupid hotshot. What do you want it for? Don't say protection. Don't say anything," I added, giving him a dirty look. "You're getting too damned picturesque." He didn't answer. "Can I have one, too?" I asked.

"No, you can have a rifle. We will go hunting together in the mountains, for wildcats."

"Like Mr. and Mrs. Palafox."

We swept past a row of almost Palladian villas, rotting and slanting perilously askew down the hill. There was something submissive in their fervent incline—something devout and not flighty—that justified Jem's words *jeunes filles bien élevées*.

"How miraculous Mexico must have looked to Cortés," Jem said. "It was grander than sixteenth-century Venice, all magical waterways alit with canoes, and palaces whose foundations were sunk deep under water. Fairy islands of flowers. Boys dressed up as grandes dames hired themselves out to the priests. (The Tlascalans agreed to give up buggering the boys if only they could keep on eating them.) And a population bigger than it was to be again for another four centuries."

But I thought that Jem wasn't listening to what he said. He seemed exultant and restless as a hummingbird, and I had to run to keep pace with him.

The town, in contrast, had that glutted stillness of Sunday afternoons in a Catholic country, a day consecrated to idleness and devotion.

We swooped down on the candy market where ladies coaxed us with spoonfuls of a goat's-milk caramel sauce that swamped the tonsils. They slapped it between two communion wafers: a holy caramel sandwich. Jem bought an entire jar of the stuff and dropped it into the tartan shopping bag already full of Mexican *Cosmopolitan* and Communist broadsheets and long pods of tamarind-and-red-chile-paste candy. We were buffeted by fat strolling families rolling down the main square like floats in the Columbus Day parade, sweating prosperity. We were heading for a park on the other side of town.

"It is the kind of park designed for you," Jem promised.

It wasn't the bandstand kind of park at all, but the one infernal place in town, the dark place above the pink scorched center, the disused mines. Above it hung a Spanish bastion, slung down the hill in careless balcony below balcony, a profusion of paved miradors and twisted columns. The fortress hung over that pitch-black park all gangly pink leopard-spotted lilies gone mad. The scent of lilies in that wildness was enough to make you dizzy just driving by. Thunderstorms had toppled umbrella pines across the white chalky paths—paths that mazed coquettishly through the humming jungle, each coming back in the end to pink fountains cracked in two. Above the pink and black park was another mirador swimming with pink scallop-shell basins. There, in the morning, the women did their washing. The talk would be the colors of the wrung-out clothes. Fuchsia nylon, turquoise shot with poison green, as if parrots had fallen screaming from the trees. There was a festering chill hanging over the park now. It was a setting for metamorphoses, the place in legend where gods would ravish girls washing their clothes, and perhaps all the mad, swaying lilies were the spirits of girls who had caught a terrible eye.

Jem did not know whose palace it had been. "Some silver racketeer's folly," he suggested without conviction. Its shaded catwalks seemed more for the patrols of mistresses than smug surveyors. I knew whoever haunted it had not come willingly. The gaping scrolled windows had bars across them which had held in imperiousness broken and starved. I could feel what it would be like to be imprisoned by someone who did not love you any more. Frightened tantrums in the night when no one came, when bells were pulled until they snapped.

"How did the Mexicans dispose of unwanted people? Was it only the firing squad?"

"They left people to their own devices sometimes. The last of Moctezuma's direct descendants through his eldest son came to Mexico when he was seventy-five years old to claim the throne of his ancestors."

"How did the Republic like that?"

"They didn't string him up—they didn't bother. He went on to New Orleans, where he blew his brains out. Over an unhappy love affair. New Orleans—Lord! Did you know that New Orleans has the only leper colony extant on this continent?"

We were lying on our stomachs among the lilies by a fountain, in the wet black dirt. Jem was pliant, full of charming irrelevancies, sweet with fatigue. Sweeter than I could remember seeing him.

"The leper colony is in Carville. There should be an opera about it. Is Carville near where your mother's family came from?"

"I shouldn't think so. They lived in Terrebonne, just across the Gulf from here. In the old photographs those Creoles look so leprous with inbreeding they're a colony unto themselves. Girls who laugh with hands over their mouths, chinless men with big eye sockets."

"Are there any real Creoles left today?" Jem asked.

"*Créole pas mouri; il desseché.* Although how they could dry up, with nothing but swamp seeping into their bones . . . Yes, a few left. Preserved, but not quite desiccated. My great-grandmother was the last pure-blood Creole in our family. Her name was Hadee Dablevert."

"Hades Greendevil," Jem repeated, thoughtfully. "Dablevert and Bocanegra: Green Devil and Blackmouth. Imagination certainly has simmered down. What Adam naming the animals would dare dole out such names today?

"Where do we go for color, Scarlet? In what corner of the soul are green devils and black mouths still manufactured? (I have a weakness for dreaming: every night a waking death in which we come to our senses, and when we wake again we lie, but one can't live in dreams.) If Adam were naming the beasts this afternoon, they'd be called by their Social Security numbers.

"The last good naming went out with the slave trade, along with high insteps and poker backs: octoroon, quadroon, mulatto, maribou, mustafino. But people got sloppy. From that fine and baroque array, choice was narrowed to the equivocal 'colored,' with its sinister and charming associations of both tainted and a child's paintbox, the still gaily exotic New World 'Negro' to dull black.

"Do you see the magic of classification? You make what you name."

"What would you call everyone if you were naming the animals?" I asked.

"I'd call us white sharks and black slugs, grandees, catamites. You and I—they named us both slave names," Jem reflected. "Why do you think that was? Did they know that we would never want to be masters?"

"Jem and Jezebel. They knew we would want to be each other's slave," I said.

In this rare, sweet mood he was willing to listen and answer instead of drilling me or ranting. I basked in his attentive euphoria, myself light-headed enough to chatter about the old slavers and my ocean liner of a great-grandmother, while he arranged my hair and held out his cheek to be stroked with childlike passivity and confidence. I was dizzy with a sense of well-being. It was going to be all right after all, by the miraculous grace of Jem's sudden disposition to be tender, to be quietly gay. A shot of the eighteenth-century virtues. We were full of non sequiturs that afternoon, like an old and happy couple.

Darkness was crashing, crashing. No weaning into pink and silver cloudlets, into twilight, but a sudden blackness that made the children spinning marbles by the fountain run away. We wandered back toward the windy hacienda in a darkness of catcalls and dogs barking and radio mariachis tuning up. We hurried along a high wet chalky road carved above the town and flanked by corrugated tin houses whose washing was strung up like Christmas lights, staring as we passed into the windows of lusciously lighted kitchens, tableaux of family life unbearably intimate and alive from the outside. Other people passed us on this high road: two schoolboys talking politics in high voices, an old couple, a grandmother and a small boy with a goat. They trudged and quarreled, spat and sang, and looked neither to the right nor the left. If it were possible to keep to such a road steadfastly looking neither right nor left, then perhaps nothing more would be required.

"I would like to paint one, and only one, exquisite painting," said Jem. "To be the Master of Saint Ursula and the Ten Thousand Virgins, Master of the Rebellious Angels. A petit-point of gold leaf and crushed lapis; paratrooper angels chasing tumbling devils, and the righteous sitting stiffly in mahogany pews above. Then nobody would bother me any more about what I was going to do with myself. If anybody asked what did Jem Chasm do, anyway, people would say, why he is the Master of the Rebellious Angels."

Before it was light the next morning Jem sent me downstairs for a bottle of Tehuacan water: he had been writing all night while I slept and he had a terrible thirst. The early morning concierge was asleep over his comic book, so I went out to the pantry and got it myself. When I came back upstairs I found Jem laid out, livid as Christ from the cross. He had put a bullet through his brain with that little black Luger and the stuffing was all knocked out of his head.

You will think that I was very cold and bad-hearted, but all I could do was curse that parched body which already looked picked bare by birds of prey. He had pulled the lowest trick yet. He had walked out on me again, pronouncing this new-born life of ours a failure, and he left me no one to whom to answer back. If I could have, I would have turned my back, pretending that I hadn't even noticed that last, wildest-craved play for attention.

Instead, I ransacked his belongings to make the reaper's

inventory. Not much was left of Jem's collection. A battered leather and wooden-spined toilet case, initialed—his Spanish grandfather's. Inside, a compass, three pairs of dark glasses, his mother's emerald necklace, my mother's ivory cross wrapped up in white flannel. Bottles of pills prescribed by Italian, Algerian, Spanish doctors: N. K. Kassim for asthma, Mr. N. P. Chass for hemorrhaging, Mr. N. J. Hassam for dizziness. An attaché case stuffed with linen, with Augustine, and an atlas.

That so rarefied and urban a creature should be confined to unhallowed Mexican scrapple, the scrubland of the Holy Roman Catholic Church, was it right? Nicolas Januarius, named for a saint who dowered poor trollops and another whose blood comes to life once a year. Truly our ends give the finger to our beginnings. I pulled open the heavy wooden shutters and above me saw a flight of Canada geese winging it south, and like them, I knew it was time to go. It seemed to me as if other people lived as if they had been plunked down in bumper cars after the power is cut, and conscience was only a reminder of the rightness that could be theirs.

I had neither conscience nor temptations. I felt the wealth of choice, the power of infinite possibility. I saw a guard of angels looking down and telling me what I did was just fine— they didn't want me up there with them when I died—while I could see the devil was raring to take me for his own. Do you say he is the creator of this world? We just try to stay out of his clutches.

But oh Jem, I wish I had stayed to see them carve you up. I would have liked to have held that raw heart in both hands. As you hold mine and will no longer, as you have given it a good tweak to make sure it's still jumping.

I leaned out the window and pointed Jem's dime-store compass. I could go back north, northeast to Louisiana to ax crocodiles and shoot craps, to the Delta where Eustacius had left behind three wives like unpaid bills and my great-grandmother's house was one black knotted thicket, singing in the night. I could go south, ever faster along dwindling latitudes, until I skidded off the earth's surface and into the Southern Cross, butting my head against the firmament. But the first order of business was clear. After disposing of Jem as the authorities saw fit, I had to get back to Casimir to whom the emeralds now belonged and who knew better than I did the answers to Jem's questions. I needed Casimir tightly now, he seemed just around the corner waiting to be whistled up, and I could already feel him getting as angry at Jem and at me as I was. I packed in a paper bag what I had chosen to take: the emeralds, the pages of cheap hotel stationery covered in his furious writing whose first word was "Jezebel," the strip of photobooth snapshots from that thieving day in Oxford, with the Chasm boys two hulking malcontents, Jem leaning against me hard and scowling, Casimir mugging like a teen ballerina. You think I wanted to remember him? No, I meant to drop that incriminating image down the nearest Mexican manhole.

There was a crumpled thousand pesos which I laid out on the bedside table for whoever was left to clean up the trouble we had caused, and a crisp deck of dollars which I took, and I kissed the backs of Jem's hands and walked out, with all the world before me and a whole lot of debts to be paid.

A NOTE ON THE TYPE

The text of this book was set in Electra, a typeface designed by W. A. Dwiggins for the Mergenthaler Linotype Company and first made available in 1935. Electra cannot be classified as either "modern" or "old style." It is not based on any historical model, and hence does not echo any particular period or style of type design. It avoids the extreme contrast between "thick" and "thin" elements that marks most modern faces, and is without eccentricities which catch the eye and interfere with reading. In general, Electra is a simple, readable typeface which attempts to give a feeling of fluidity, power, and speed.

Composed by Graphic Composition Co., Inc., Athens, Georgia.

Printed and bound by Haddon Craftsmen, Inc.,
Scranton, Pennsylvania.

Typography and binding design by Virginia Tan.